The Wine Cork Collector

STORIES

by

JAMES I. MCGOVERN

WingSpan Press

Published in the United States and the United Kingdom by WingSpan Press, Livermore, CA

The WingSpan name, logo and colophon are the trademarks of WingSpan Publishing.

ISBN 978-1-59594-627-0 (pbk.)
ISBN 978-1-59594-941-7 (ebk.)

First edition 2018

Printed in the United States of America

www.wingspanpress.com

Library of Congress Control Number 2018954663

1 2 3 4 5 6 7 8 9 10

A free man is one who lives under the guidance of reason,
who is not led by fear,
but who directly desires that which is good.

--Spinoza, *Ethics*

CONTENTS

THE LONER AS CHILD

My memory of Uptown Chicago, '51 to '53, is infused with a toxic haze. Coal was being burned, food being fried through open windows, autos and trucks emitting raw fumes, small industry thriving among old apartment buildings. In summer the overgrown trees shed their fragrance, as did flowers lining the bricks and weeds choking the useless half-lot next to our building. But the haze in my memory is also a product of time. Not only of its long passage since then, but of the point in history of that period. The world war had been over less than a decade, its destruction and horror still vivid, with a lesser war already going on, as well as threats for down the road. A mood of relief but of sorrow, and of hope but of fear seemed to hang in the air, at least among the adults of that time.

The majority of people in our neighborhood were Jewish, but my family was Catholic and belonged to Our Lady of Lourdes parish. The church and school were about half a mile south. As a first-grader I'd return from classes with my older sister, mostly along a cemetery wall bordering Clark Street. We lived on Argyle, which was just north of the cemetery and ran about two blocks between Clark and Broadway to the east. Our building was about halfway down Argyle, across from where a small intersecting street ran south a short block to the cemetery wall. There was a larger lot to one side at that point, with a dilapidated fence and large piles of sand inside, a faded *Keep Out* sign posted.

Walking with my sister, or with one of my parents past the shops along Clark, I was essentially an automaton. I followed and obeyed instinctively, my every move in concordance with theirs. Everything was controlled, purposeful. But at some point I was out on my own, not just in the space around our building, but beyond its iron fence. I was usually with Bobby, a friend my age from the much bigger building next door. His building had enclosed gangways, great for running through while shouting as loud as one could, no doubt to people's annoyance. Bobby knew other boys in his building, but they didn't seem to like me, or Bobby himself when he was with me. His father was friendly, though, when I'd see him. He'd give us huge kosher pickles from his delivery truck parked on the street. He smiled when I first tasted one and reacted to the hot taste.

There were times with Bobby when we'd get into mischief. The janitor in his building had some large brown beer bottles accumulating, and a boy said they could be redeemed for deposit refunds. We took the bottles to the corner tavern and, sure enough, received some change for them. The coins felt very satisfying in my hand. But the janitor found us out and angrily demanded the money, which of course we yielded. More successful was a flower-picking escapade down the street towards Broadway. We were collecting the flowers to sell when a middle-aged woman came out of the building scolding us. We took off running and Bobby and I escaped, but the woman was able to catch a smaller boy who was with us. She made him take her to his family, who lived back near the tavern. We sold the flowers outside a theater on Broadway.

There was eventually an incident that cost Bobby and me our friendship, a sundering unfair to both of us, yet perhaps inevitable. We were sitting on the back steps outside Bobby's apartment, a couple of other boys with us. One was an older boy, thick-set and aggressive, and he was handling a plastic table knife with serrated edge. I was somewhat used to this boy and didn't fear him, or the type of knife he held. But he wondered aloud if it really cut, then suddenly seized my arm and began sawing above the wrist. I was surprised and didn't react at first, but pulled away when he increased the pressure. I saw a straight red mark around a slight scratch in my skin. There wasn't much pain but I sensed something was wrong and departed.

Later, my mother noticed me examining the mark and asked what had happened. I told her matter-of-factly and she said to stay in until my father came home. I was in the parlor when he arrived, and as he talked with my mother in the kitchen, out of my hearing. But the next thing I knew I was being seized by the arm and marched down the steps of our building. Once on the street, my father had me direct him to Bobby's apartment. So it was down the familiar gangway, around the many wooden stairways, and then up several flights to Bobby's back door. No one was around outside, so my father banged aggressively on the door until Bobby's father, the pickle truck driver, opened it a few inches and peered out. I watched as he nodded confusedly, trying to smile and be friendly, as my father delivered a lengthy harangue. I didn't hear a word of it since I was enveloped in shame.

I was confined thereafter to the space around our building unless accompanied by my sister. She had a friend from school in the neighborhood who also had younger siblings, so I joined their little group. This led to a serious incident in the sand piles near the cemetery. Some of us were playing in there, despite the *Keep Out* sign, and I was looking to hide as part of a game. I unexpectedly found a hole near some rusty equipment and jumped in, all the while looking back. As I turned my head toward the shadowy side of the hole I saw a gray, crumpled man staring fixedly at me. My child's mind could not comprehend the lack of movement, the lack of life. A primitive instinct asserted itself, however, and I was quickly out of the hole, running with fear from the hitherto unknown.

I passed my sister and her friend who were talking on the sidewalk, ran the short block to Argyle Street and across, surprised my mother who was busy in the apartment. She was somewhat vexed by my garbled account but alerted by my description of the dead man's stare. She made the requisite call to police, then led me back to the scene in the sand piles.

I recall people milling about, most being kept away from the hole. A uniformed policeman towered above me in the sun, smiling as he asked if I'd discovered the body, about when, and what I'd been doing there. My mother was beside me but I saw only the policeman. He soon nodded and said something to her, turning away then to the hole. Some men in plain work clothes were moving a covered bundle into a dark van.

My memory of the incident ends at that point. I can't recall the evening, or the days immediately following. There was a problem with dreams, and I never went near the sand piles again, in fact only playing next to our building. I preferred to stay indoors. I had a younger brother who became my only playmate, something that couldn't begin to work out. I was blamed for every problem he had, or seemed to have, and of course any injury. We jumped up from supper one night and ran through the apartment, he tripping on a rug wrinkle and hitting his head on a radiator. He had to be taken to a hospital for stitches, my father incensed beyond words. The whole family went in the car, nobody speaking, I cowering in humiliation.

We moved out of Uptown soon after, and out of the city entirely. Our new home, a house, was on a four-lane blacktop without sidewalks, just gravel shoulders. A dense growth of forest was across the road for as far as we could see. It was a month or two into the school year so my sister and I had a sudden adjustment to make.

The old city neighborhood would retreat into memory, perhaps for the better in my case. The haze engulfing it would thicken, veiling and distorting the details, the faces. And yet some light of warning shone through, a check on the boyish impulse to run. My view outward turned inward. Caution took hold, not easing when it should but sometimes slipping when it shouldn't. Not quite predictable. Thus emerged the pattern for my ensuing life.

⊕⊢ᴈ⊰⊱Ͼⵏⵏⵕ

After the move, we took a yellow bus to school through our amorphous, undeveloped suburb. It was a novel switch from our walks along the cemetery wall. My sister's responsibility for me was greatly reduced, so she was freer to develop her own friendships. The parish school was of recent construction and single-story, in stark contrast to the nineteenth-century monolith we'd attended in the city. There was only one bus, so it made multiple trips and we had to wait every day to get home. The bus waiters hung around or played in the church parking lot. In bad weather we were moved to the church basement, rather cramped since the church was small and outdated. The group could become restless then, and I recall some older girls breaking into a song that stuck in my memory:

Who's the meanest nun of all?
Virrr-ginette!
Who gets me up against the wall?
Virrr-ginette!
She leans at me, she screams at me,
She gives me extra his-to-ry!
Virgy Virgy Vir-gin-ette!

I was to have this nun as my teacher five years later, for seventh grade, then again for eighth when another nun became disabled. In the meantime I had the older students' sentiments to consider.

For a while my mother would lay out my play clothes for my return from school. It would be late afternoon, due to the bus delay, and so quite a relief to change out of my school uniform and dress shoes. It was warm that first autumn and I recall running in denim shorts through the leaf-strewn back yard, my little brother in tow. I didn't venture further, however, into the neighborhood behind us or the prairie down the block. The old prohibition from the city remained imprinted on my mind. In addition, I was forbidden to cross the blacktop into the forest facing our house.

The winter was quite harsh, with heavy snow and heating issues. My brother and I slept in the unfinished attic, with no direct heat. The chimney ran through and the door at the foot of the stairs was left open, but, on extreme nights, with the wind howling and rattling the windows at both ends, it seemed we were more outside than in. It puzzled me how my brother fell asleep before I did, but this distraction let me forget the cold and drop off myself.

The school bus was also unheated except by the driver's seat, with an ice-fringed sheet of water in the aisle. The school itself, though of recent construction, also had heating problems so we often wore our coats in class. The Christmas break was especially welcome that year. Our presents were on the modest side, but I received a "Lincoln Logs" set that aroused and held my interest. The chubby brown cylinders and thin green slats could only be formed into a few meaningful structures, but I persisted in seeking more. The very limitations of the log set whetted my appetite for more complex tools with which to test my abilities, and to know the world impersonally. Thus, in future Christmases, I'd be absorbed in "Erector" sets, first basic and then advanced, assembling a multitude of metal pieces into almost as many objects. When I eventually felt the tedium of such play, I moved on to assembling and painting plastic models of things. The vehicle, ship, airplane, or rocket would then sit on display in our attic room, an assurance that I could master some things.

But in the meantime the years passed slowly, especially during summertime. The heat in our upstairs room was often intolerable, so the cool basement was a welcome refuge, card games with siblings the chief activity. On better days I'd sit at an attic window watching boys at play in "The Field," the wild prairie at the end of our block. I had no desire to join them, yet I felt some vague affinity, so I'd keep score during their ball games. It never occurred to me that there was anything strange in sitting isolated and occupied this way.

There was only one house on our block between ours and The Field. In their yard I'd see Adelle, who was a year younger than me, playing with her little niece, whose family lived on the street behind us. I found watching them a nice break from spying on ball games. Of course, I'd also encounter Adelle outside, but it seemed at first she should be my sister's friend, not mine. Their age difference asserted itself, however, as my sister made friends at school, so the gender barrier relaxed between Adelle and me. I'd wander over and enjoy being with her, not doing anything special, just finding something peaceful and natural in her physical nearness, her open expression. She had very light blue eyes that I found hypnotic.

I recall once, in an elevated mood, I picked Adelle up in my arms and spun around, giving her a ride. It hurt a bit, but it was worth the hurt to see her face, feel her joy. That was in the open, on her front lawn. I preferred to be entirely alone with her. We lay under the bushes on occasion, spying on the world though there wasn't much to see. Once, after we'd hidden in her basement eating ripe bananas, her mother was angry since she'd planned to bake bread with them. Her parents were mostly tolerant, though. Her father even paid me to water their lawn while they were on vacation. I watered liberally, watching dead locusts float in a stream under the bushes, thinking of Adelle. We took a long walk in The Field after she returned.

I continued in solitary activities even while enjoying my new friendship. I'd received a microscope and was permitted to cross the blacktop to collect specimens from the forest ponds. I viewed the one-celled creatures with fascination, inviting others to also look, not at first noticing their weaker interest. Even Adelle's reaction was subdued, as if she didn't understand my enthusiasm. They were just germs to her. When I later received a chemistry set, I didn't bring her to our basement to watch the experiments. She had her own interests, of course. As we grew older she collected movie star cards that were sold in packs at the dime store. I pretended to be interested, though it was only part pretense since I enjoyed her own interest. We'd watch old movies on television in their basement, there being no theater nearby, and sometimes she'd squirm against me. She wanted to kiss me once during a kissing scene in the movie and I had to comply, or thought I had to. This led to an awkward explanation at my weekly Confession that Saturday.

My parents were mostly silent about my friendship with Adelle, though suggestions were made about playing with other boys. As it happened, a coworker of one of my uncles moved to our town with his family, which included a boy my own age who entered my class at school. He was outgoing, good at sports, and it was expected by the adults that we'd be friends. He was frequently at our house, which offended my older sister since he made smart remarks and swung his fists about by way of greeting. He became for me someone to tolerate. This was sometimes hard, though, such as when he'd want to "fight for fun" outside. We'd get so dirty rolling in the dust I'd be required to take a bath before having supper. This did, however, provide amusement for my sister.

In "fighting for fun," my assigned friend and I were about equally matched in size and strength. But though I often got him in holds that should have won the fight, he refused to "give" and I'd eventually release him out of boredom. The fight would then continue until I myself "gave," often again simply to escape the tedium. This prefigured an indifference toward winning that would limit my later efforts in competition. Much of what I'd see people striving for would not seem worth the strain and anxiety. And from this assessment, unfortunately, it was a short mental step to concluding that most people were stupid.

❖❖❖❖❖

My deep-seated drift toward isolation naturally induced me to become an avid reader. I preferred the boys' adventure books and would spend whatever money I had acquiring the Hardy Boys series. Once read, a book would join its fellows in an unmoving procession on the shelf, awaiting my brother's graduation from comic books. I read other things as well, but what would seem a positive habit was met with indifference by my parents. While maybe better than playing with a girl, more normal than peering at pond water, it was still not the gregarious display of a "real boy." But I couldn't care less about all that. Reading gave me an escape from mundanity, and when a taste for the exotic arose I expanded to stamp collecting. The images and fine engraving gave me an appreciation of other places and times, to be enjoyed in the dark intimacy of the private world I nurtured.

Stamp collecting involved buying through the mail, which I found enjoyable, so I was soon ordering many other items as well. Mistakes were sometimes made. Once when I'd ordered a telescope, the company sent me a dagger, my mother almost fainting when I showed it to her. Not long after this, she encouraged me to save for a camera, a more useful item that would provide a more mature pastime. This stemmed the flow of mail orders, but also led to my acquisition of darkroom equipment. The development and printing of images, whatever the subjects, by my own hand in the red-lit gloom of our basement, was a pleasure that transcended the simple taking of pictures. It was partly the darkness and privacy of the activity, as before, but also the move away from passivity. I was making something happen. And it was something from the world of adults, their hobby or even their profession. In the darkroom I was a grown-up.

At school, having advanced into the upper grades, I naturally sought to distance myself from younger students. This involved dispensing with the school bus and traveling the two miles to school on foot. While this wasn't unusual for older students, especially boys, my distance to walk was the longest among the students. It could be challenging when the weather was wet or wintry, but once committed I could not go back. My parents had discontinued paying my bus fee. I developed a very fast walk to stay warm or reach shelter from the rain, not running except for a sort of jog in deep snow. My caution toward running hung on from earlier life, but the fast walk kicked in even if not needed, some of my peers taking note. The term "Crazylegs" came to be used.

My sense of maturity was strengthened for a while by a weekly activity I shared with my parents. A big Chicago newspaper ran a crossword puzzle contest with a thousand dollars for the correct solution. It appeared each Sunday with the submission deadline a day or two later. The previous week's solution was beside the new puzzle, along with explanations of why the words shown were correct. Since many of the letters were pre-printed on the puzzle, there would be only two or three words that might match a given "clue." The explanations of correct choices were often abstruse, arbitrary, and evocative of groans from my parents. There were few winners in the contest, often none, with any leftover prize added to the one for the following week. Nonetheless, I enjoyed a rare, fulfilling sort of camaraderie with my parents, each of us preparing our individual entry for the new contest. I myself came the closest to winning, once missing just a single word, my mother looking wistful as she mulled the explanation.

Another feature in the Sunday paper was the history quiz, five questions with the answers upside-down at the bottom. The quiz was embedded in a short column written by a pictured professor. He did not write the questions himself, but paid five dollars apiece to the readers who'd sent them in. With my extra reading and information from stamp collecting, besides what I gleaned at school, I easily came up with endless questions which I submitted profusely. I fully expected to have multiple acceptances and a nice little income. No response was forthcoming, however. I didn't understand this since, besides there being less competition than with the crossword, the published questions often seemed quite dull to me. I even noticed an error in one of the answers, about which I wrote to the professor. Again there was no response. I quit reading the column then, taking a dim view of historians thereafter.

The professor must have known that I was a kid, perhaps thought he'd hurt his status by dealing with me. I sensed something was wrong at the time but didn't know what. I thought maybe I'd been rash, run again when I should have walked. If I was to enter an adult activity it had to be with adults' approval, their partnership. I soon got my chance at the weekly bingo games held at a local banquet hall. My mother had wanted to attend but my sister declined to accompany her, so I went instead. The hall was surprisingly full, most of the players women with multiple bingo cards before them. I saw a couple of elderly men, two or three girls from school, but otherwise felt the oddball. With my mother's help, however, I was soon into the game, even drinking coffee since that and tea were all they had. As the games droned on, a woman at our table noticed that I had bingo, became excited, and did the shouting for me. My mother sent me up through the staring crowd to collect my prize, which turned out to be a bath towel.

I still felt a pull toward solitude, fast-walking past people in the community, my interest drawn to new activities but not the people who were in them. This displaced my collecting phase, which reduced my passivity, so in a way I advanced. But the lack of social engagement was there and bred a sense of alienation. I recalled my friendship with Adelle, and Bobby before her, and wondered why an invisible wall now stood between me and such closeness. At the same time, being a kid, I felt powerless to change things. But then something happened.

It was following sixth grade, as I recall, which would make it 1958. My father, perhaps still rankled by my personality, arranged for me and my brother to go to a sports camp run by an order of religious brothers. It was a goodly distance from home, near the border with Wisconsin. I was signed up for four weeks and my brother for two. I saw little of him there since we were in different age groups, each group in its own barracks-like "cabin." The camp was in part of a huge estate donated to the brothers by an old robber baron upon his death. There was a luxurious mansion on the far side of the property where we'd go to use the swimming pool. Once, while changing, I wandered into the residence and saw sumptuous fixtures and furnishings, high ceilings with old-fashioned portraits on the walls.

Part of our walk to the mansion was across a vast grassy area originally tended as a lawn. The brothers informed us that it was the largest private lawn in the world. On the end opposite the mansion was a private lake with boathouse, then the woods leading to our camp. The big lawn had seen lavish outdoor parties in another era, but for us campers it was just a useless void before the pool. One of the sports brothers decided to change that, however, and had the campers from the older boys' cabin assemble for a footrace. It was late in the day, perhaps even after our evening meal. A golden glow emanated from the west, the sun close to setting, with a wide, violet-tinged sky above. The brother pointed to an enormous tree across the expanse of grass, saying the race would be around that tree and back, no cutting in front of it allowed. He had us take our marks.

The shout was given and we all surged forward, many flagging in the longish grass, not mowed as often as in the robber baron's day. Conditioned by my jogging in snow, however, I managed the grass by lifting my knees high. I led the pack as we crossed the heart of the estate. Approaching the great tree, I hit a drier stretch with sparser grass and lengthened my lead. I swung around the tree unmolested, no other runners present to hinder or distract me. I sprinted away as the pack slowed for the turn. I heard angry shouts from confusion at the tree, runners no doubt bumping and tripping each other, but I focused on the distant finish line where Brother stood with his arms folded. Hitting again the longer grass, I became aware of a runner close enough to me that I could hear his breathing. He was soon within my peripheral vision and I stole a glance at him.

He was not a camper but a high school boy who'd assisted around the camp. He was apparently staying with the brothers for the summer, deciding whether he would join them. I hadn't paid him much notice. Now, however, as he inched up and drew even with me, he became for the moment the center of my universe. I wanted to win. I'd thought I had the race won but that was premature. I had to beat this runner at my side no matter who he was, no matter what it took. I kept my knees high and kicked at the stubborn grass with piston-like thrusts. My rival was laboring. I lifted my gaze to the sky, feeling strong and ready to win, and yet his body was slightly ahead.

He leaned forward at the finish, unnecessarily, as if there was a tape to break. We slowed side-by-side as if out for a casual run.

"He almost beat you," Brother addressed the winner.

The young man looked down, still breathing hard.

"You're not staying up too late, are you?"

"He's just fast," the winner shrugged.

The others were coming in with banter and arguments, someone complaining to Brother about being held by the tree. The high school boy approached me.

"Are you on track at your school?"

"They don't have it yet."

He nodded.

"It's a great sport." Then, as he turned away: "Good race."

The sun was hidden on the horizon and twilight poised to set in. The old mansion seemed to be dissolving in mists. Brother gave a shout or two and our amorphous band headed back to camp. For most of the boys it had been just another activity, another ordinary day. But I had a sense that it was special.

At the end of the camp session, awards were given out to the top participants in the regular activities. They were leather plaques, hand-made and inscribed by the brother who taught crafts, our lone non-sports activity. Though I'd been mediocre in most of the activities, I still received the overall award for "Sportsman of the Trip," the top prize. Along with everyone else, I knew it was for the race. I realized I wasn't alone in seeing its importance.

❦┄❈┄❈┄❦

That autumn, I entered seventh grade and had the dreaded Sister Virginette as my teacher. She was in fact strict, a quality exaggerated by her tallness, but many of my classmates had grown flippant and so elicited her harshness. I myself had no problem with her, no doubt helped by my sister's having been an excellent student. The halo effect could reach far, as I'd learned from the race at camp, and one day Sister Virginette told me that I'd make an excellent priest. I duly went on the tour of seminaries with our pastor and several other boys, but I saw from my parents' negative reaction that the idea was doomed. I never knew precisely why.

I quit my fast-walking, assuming a normal gait unless there was reason to hurry. Speed was to be used selectively. I also tried to be less conspicuous as a loner. I was helped in this when I was given the chore of burning trash in our backyard. I don't recall why this was necessary, but for me it provided less obvious private times. The smoke might well have been unhealthy, but rising in the chill air it softened my immediate reality. I was able to view all the pieces coming together, the sequence of events that had brought me to the reflective moment I now enjoyed. My memories ran back to Uptown, where we'd previously lived, but at that point there was smoke again, or haze, so that I couldn't see farther back.

FIRST CLASS CITIZENS

As the young woman approached the end of a short line, she noticed a young man standing nearby. He too was holding papers like those she needed to file.

"Are you in line?" she asked.

He gave a slight start. He'd been looking about the great hall and his mind had apparently wandered.

"No. I was lingering a bit. Loitering." He smiled. "Go ahead. You're next."

She took the next place in line, conscious of his continuing to view her. She wore a raincoat over her office clothes, had longish dark blond hair, and wore glasses with clear plastic frames.

"Guess I'll get in line now," came his voice.

She glanced back at him. He was on the tall side and dark-haired. He had an air of indecisiveness about him, a vulnerable smile, as if he were a poet or social worker misplaced in the business world.

They waited but the line didn't move. Though there were a dozen service windows, only three had their lights on, one of which had no clerk present. The rest of the great hall was almost empty. A few vendors idly stood, someone now and then crossed between street and elevators.

"Slow today," he finally said.

"It is whenever I come," she replied.

"Me too, actually. And every three months. Seems it needn't be that often. How much can change in that time?"

"Tell me about it. But what can you do? It's an awful lot better than the alternative."

"Yeah, for sure. There's no substitute for citizenship."

A man ahead of them was impatient and left. Soon after, the absent clerk returned and the line grew still shorter. The two young people would soon be separated.

"Like to stop for coffee after?" he asked.

She looked back at him again, noncommittally.

"Well, I'm working."

"Me too. Perhaps a glass of wine, then."

Her eyes locked onto his, a smile beginning.

"Coffee," she said. "And I'm Louise."

"Peter," he replied.

There was a restaurant just a short distance away. As they were walking to it, they saw three youths in garish clothes on the opposite side of the street, being questioned by police. An armored police van waited at the curb.

"Clean-up time," Louise commented.

"I hear they're using the punishment more."

"They have to. If you just take L3s back they're soon on your street again."

They continued on to the restaurant, which was bland in appearance and dimly lit. A neatly printed sign on the door attracted their attention. It read:

Applications Being Taken
Citizens Only, Level 2 and Up

"Want to change jobs?" Peter joked.

"Not today."

They sat at a table and were served by a woman with

chestnut bangs and bright eyes. She took care of herself, Louise thought, but still had the non-reflective look of the L2s. Better than Level 3, of course, that turbid sea of emotion.

"Know any off-levels?" she asked Peter.

He was taken aback at first, then glanced toward the sign on the door.

"Actually," he said, "my younger sister's an L2. She didn't like school so she skipped university. But she has a nice enough job, works in the Data Capital."

"Oh, good for her. But there's instability near there. Don't you worry about her?"

"No. The guards are top-rate and the police like here. The L3s aren't so bad and any Roamers they see are fried on sight."

"Seems they'd know enough to stay out."

"They're basically just animals. They think of something they want, they sneak in from the Wastes to steal. But then–ZAP! End of problem."

"It might get tough for her, though, your sister. There's the no-children law, L2 and down. Didn't your family try to talk to her?"

"Oh, of course. But she was the last of us five so, well, I guess my parents let her drift a bit."

Louise studied him. He was a sincere type, more like a monk than a poet or social worker. Working in business must be torture for him.

"I don't know," Peter said, "maybe things will ease up soon. If it's simply a question of numbers, we must be getting more predominant."

"You think it can be achieved, then? Purification?"

"Well, that's the basic idea, isn't it? The point of all this? We have our Constitution and all."

"Sure, as a standard, a working theory, but—"

He looked pained and she stopped, felt a need to change tack.

"The thing is," she continued, "there's the Roamers, breeding like rabbits out in the Wastes. You can't destroy them *all*. And with off-level citizens, L3s as well as L2s, there's that thing about *needing* a certain number. Economics, the gene pool—"

"You don't think they're serious about it, then? About purification?"

"Not entirely. Not for during our lifetimes."

He sat back and she liked what she saw: a man thinking. It was something unfamiliar to her.

"Peter," she said, "did you want to ask me out somewhere?"

❦⊱⋇⊰❦

The old opera house was nearly empty, but a formal string quartet was playing at center stage, directed by a tall slender man with long silvery locks. Louise and Peter sat in choice seats on the main floor, as did a few dozen other people. The lighting was dim and would occasionally flicker. As the musicians rested from a challenging work, their director turned to address the sparse audience.

"As I peer into this near-void, I'm reminded of the words of a writer from long ago. He said through one of his characters that a true work of art is static, isolated, and set apart from the world. Thus, an artist too might be cut off from the rest of the world. It is natural in the attainment of true art.

"Now, while this is no doubt true in some cases, to apply it here tonight would be indulging in self-consolation. I'm afraid the arts have fallen on lean times. Well, if they're to be preserved for an elite, or as a class symbol, so be it. Consider yourselves as special as you wish, friends, for you are very special to *us*. We will continue to work hard as your partners in propping up a culture."

He turned back to the musicians, launched them into a

spirited piece that defied the great empty space before them. Louise listened attentively, conscious of the music's importance to Peter, not only as art but also as something he could share with her. She would let him do this, share with her, and see how long it lasted, this connection that was different and better than what she'd known before. He wasn't fully aware of himself, she thought, but it wasn't his fault. It was the flawed and inescapable nature of their time, their period of history. Maybe she could help him.

The performance soon ended and the onlookers filed out, their footsteps distinct in the once-grand lobby, muted as they entered the drizzle and light wind of evening. Umbrellas popped up and the art lovers dispersed to their secure neighborhoods. Peter and Louise huddled close as they walked.

"Nice to be able to park so close," he commented. "It gets easier and easier with the car-owning restrictions."

"Score one for the Plan," said Louise.

He smiled down at her.

"Yes, a sign of progress. Good things to come."

They stopped to have wine at a candlelit pub. It had popcorn on the tables, something Louise didn't care for, though peanuts were worse. There was moody piano music a ways off, Peter nodding to it uncertainly. There weren't many other people and conversation was low.

"Do you get out of the city much?" she asked.

"Not much, no. If I'm gone too long they encroach on my accounts."

She nodded in token sympathy.

"That's a problem I don't have. Nobody's looking for more work at NMA."

"You're in pretty solid there?"

"Well, my husband worked there before he died. I guess there's a permanent sympathy for me, though I wish there wasn't."

"It must have been rough for you, though."

"Actually, no. He was sick and incurable and opted for Early Exit. My only thought was to help him through, deal rightly with what had to be."

"What about his family?"

"Opposed at first, then not so much when they saw the financial reality."

"Something like the End of Life options."

"Yes, though it's easier to accept the Exit when you're 75. You avoid those Decrepit Life fines, too. With us he was young but he'd have all those bills."

Peter looked away reflectively.

"The expenses, the suffering. Early Exit the right answer. Nothing much else except the Wastes."

"Not really an option."

"No. Not at all."

Louise waited, let his thoughts run their course as he stared at the table.

"That is our world," he said without looking up.

She waited a moment, then reached across the table and took his hand.

"Why don't you let me make dinner for you tomorrow?"

⊕⊣β⊃∣¢⋅Ɛ⊢⊛

The day had been colder than expected, and windy, with occasional bursts of ineffectual sunshine. Louise would normally have a long walk on her day off, but today settled for a trip to the market. There was Peter's visit to prepare for. The thought had possessed her since early that morning, bringing extra refreshment as she showered. It was a break from the routine. Now, however, a slight anxiety crept in, as if she should be wary of something going wrong. She therefore bought pre-cooked beef—a professional's work—and selected tiny potatoes to steam, they more expensive than ever. For a vegetable she thought mushrooms would do. The wine selection was quite limited, but she found a middle-priced red that looked inviting.

While her building was on the shoreline, Louise's apartment faced away from the water. Seventeen floors up, she could view the city for a considerable distance, though she did not often do so. Today would be different. With Peter as her guest, the panorama below would provide just the right ambience for their time together. They could relax in their own bubble of time above the grinding realities of their century. Sunset would be especially nice.

A call from lobby security announced his arrival. He was soon at her door, chocolates in hand, looking amazed at the dressy self she presented.

"Good evening," he said formally.

She ushered him in with mock ceremony. He looked around the apartment as if impressed. She took his raincoat.

"I'll give you the tour," she said.

It was only a few steps in each direction. He seemed vaguely amused by the bedroom, as if unaccustomed to the feminine touches. She left his raincoat on the bed.

"Shall we have a couple of shell breakers?" she offered.

He again showed surprise, as if making cocktails would be a feat for her.

"Just one for me," he said.

Her mouth opened but she didn't speak, loath to explain that "couple" had meant one apiece. She smiled at him and went to the kitchen area.

"It's a nice craft whiskey," she said as she brought the drinks.

He answered by taking too big a sip. His eyes widened.

"Too strong?"

"No, it's fine."

"It has a little more punch than the traditionals."

He was seated on one side of the love seat with a full view of the city, she in a chair in the direction of the kitchen. She'd move to the love seat once dinner was out of the way.

"So what did you study at university?" he asked.

"Biology," she smiled. "I had a dream about getting into medical practice. Not much connection to my work now, of course. How about you?"

"History. I guess it gave me some understanding of things, how they got this way. You have to trust what they tell you, of course."

"Not much choice."

He nodded, sipping whiskey. They were silent a moment.

"Lights are coming on," she said.

They stood and moved to the large window. Familiar lines and clusters of lights were marking the streets and plazas of the city, piercing the twilight. The Level 3 zone, just visible in the distance, was distinctly dimmer. Only a blue glow along the barrier matched the lighting of the city proper. Beyond the city, of course, was darkness, broken only by fortified highways and the campfires of Roamers.

"Beautiful," she said, "isn't it?"

"Yes. The order, the sense of purpose."

She sensed him turning his head to look at her, felt his hand taking hers. Her heart picked up a little as she saw things were going right. She turned to meet his eyes, felt her face glowing, saw him smile in response.

"The dinner's ready," she said.

They sat down to their simple repast. She'd lit candles and put on music while he waited, and now sliced a loaf of cranberry bread she'd decided to add. He watched her with such a fond expression that she stopped to look at him.

"My grandmother used to make that," he said. "A real long time ago, of course, on the old family farm. Roamers are in there now, but my brother still holds title. With the Plan, maybe, someday—"

Louise smiled sympathetically, kept slicing.

"These are great potatoes," he said later. "Hard to get now, I'll bet."

"Yes, the unforgiving climate. But I've been lucky. My market has an 'in' with Distribution."

"That's good. It's good to get an edge now when you can."

Louise silently agreed, and for reasons Peter would share though they weren't discussable yet. She hated being on her own now, the dead apartment, the empty space in the bed. She was nagged by the little mail holder with upright bills addressed only to her. She had her job, yes, her social status, and had nothing to complain about by the standards of the Controllers. But it was all rather fragile when you looked beyond the provisional structures of society and planet economy. The Plan was still on alert against rage from beneath and jealousy from the margins. The L1 was expected to function on her own, to compete, then advance as she merited. But this might require an edge beyond the official, the statistical. For Louise this meant an alliance, two people instead of one, united against the whims of history, the evil history in which they were living.

"There's no dessert," she said, "but I have a liqueur. It's chartreuse."

"Really? How did you manage that?"

"From my boss at work. I don't know where he got it."

She'd saved it for a special occasion, which she wouldn't say but Peter might sense on his own.

"Shall we move to the living room?" she said when she'd poured the chartreuse.

She turned the music up slightly before joining him on the love seat. It was fully dark outside, the city lights looking sharper, less delicate.

"To us," Peter toasted, and Louise clinked her glass to his.

"This is lovely," he added after they'd sipped.

His use of the word distracted her. There was nothing wrong with it, she knew, but she was unaccustomed to hearing it from a man. Of course, she'd also been unaccustomed to his thoughtfulness, his sensitivity. So it was a package deal, like always. To gain something you wanted, a bunch of positives, you had to accept a few flaws along the way.

"Yes," she said to him, "I will cherish it."

"Cherish," he repeated rather woozily, staring into space. "Yes, we have much to be grateful for."

"I was thinking mostly of now, you and I here together."

He looked down at her, focusing with some effort.

"Of course. Our position here, our being able to be here like this. It's valuable. It must always be protected."

"And used." She'd almost added "passionately," but refused to wax archaic.

"Yes, used," he agreed flatly.

"*Really* used," she ventured.

He was hooked. He tentatively put an arm around her, moved toward her face—her lips now raised—and they fell together into the archaic yet eternal vortex.

⊸⊹⊱⊰⊹⊶

Louise lay in her bed, Peter asleep beside her. She was on her back, he nestled against her, his arm lying on her torso. The clothes they'd been wearing were draped over objects in the room. There was faint light from out in the kitchen.

Yes, she thought, it was a good night. The first in a really long while. That emptiness since the death, the horror of illness before, the distance everyone had kept and how could she blame them? She'd wanted to end it so much herself and any old way would do. She'd been cruel at the end in her thoughts, but why should she be ruined? Why should her whole life be ruined? She'd come from a good family, decent anyway, and done her part with them and in school. She deserved as much as anyone else. Deserved. Hah! As if that meant anything now.

She looked down at his arm on her.

That interminable kissing before, mundane comments in the intervals. Fondling as if they were children. She'd again sounded blunt when she suggested the bedroom. But it was no problem for him, her directness. He was a nice guy—too nice some would say, a little soft. She'd cover for him with the family, make him likeable. There'd be inheritance someday, with two sisters and the cousin who'd lived with them. Competition.

It had been awkward here at first. Was he inexperienced? Maybe just the new partner, anxieties from outside. It had ended well, though, a certain subtlety there that she found gratifying. She could have kissed some more then but it was over for him and he slept. For her it was a new beginning, a portal opening, so she stayed awake looking in. She wanted to forget the past and its residue that polluted the present.

The warmest memories were of earliest times, before her awareness began of the weakness of the economy and the instability, the threat of anarchy, behind it. The sudden reduction of comforts, of holiday gifts, then their cautious restoration, accompanied by steeled acceptance of hateful, necessary realities. To the maturing girl so much had seemed arbitrary—the severe restrictions on companions, on dress, and the curfews, forbidden areas, physical boundaries of civilization. Her cousin and her first husband had gone beyond them in national service, her cousin returning unscathed but her husband with something that killed him. Always that smothering priority of security, harsh laws and social values that defied the old leanings toward liberality, leanings now discredited. Their legacy was those creatures out in the Wastes.

She sometimes envied the women of Level 2, their freedom

from higher expectations, from children or the decision whether to have them. But then she caught herself. To be tempted toward inferior existence was encroaching insanity. The common feeling toward Level 2 was tolerant irritation, while humans at Level 3 were simply aggravating, parasites who drained resources and shackled progress. They couldn't be trusted and were therefore a threat to safety and stability.

Louise lifted Peter's arm off her and turned onto her side, facing away from him.

There'd been aloneness, of course, and that was part of the reason this was happening. But it could never be the main thing, the controlling reason. That was one of the myths of the past, along with overpowering love and the need to have children. So many absurdly sentimental things had once been taken for granted. There must have been *some* knowledge that practical alliance was the sanest course, but people had lacked the courage to admit it. Along with many other things. Such silly forebears they'd had. But all that was being changed now, supposedly toward Purification. She doubted it would be achieved but it had to be the standard. Strength and power were their most necessary values. Blast all the Roamers, keep the L3s invisible. Optimal happiness through quality in people. Yes.

Louise fell asleep thinking of Peter at her side.

HOUR OF THE CATS

Even before his leopard-skin loincloth was delivered, Arnold was making his midnight rounds. He'd walk along the boundaries of the properties, meeting only the occasional cat, as he studied the backyards and windows of his bourgeois neighbors. He could range for blocks since he was sly crossing streets. And that was where the appeal lay, after all: the being unseen while yet he was seeing. It gave him a sense of power to balance his usual vulnerability, the scrutiny he received at the office, on the train, and in his home. He was master of the night during this pre-sleep interlude.

It had begun as a simple stroll when Heidi would go to bed early. She'd been put on full-time at the arboretum, working in the herbarium, and she took her work very seriously. The arbitrary bedtime with Arnold had to be sacrificed. He remained in his old amorphous pattern, not wishing to change, and filled the void of her absence with indifferent activities. Hence arose his walk to take the night air, first up and down the street but soon shifting to less conventional, aberrant routes.

It occurred to him early on, when he left the street to walk the rear boundaries of yards, that he needn't take care in dressing as he usually did. Indeed, it might be better if he weren't recognizable. Not that he was likely to be seen. He could probably wear anything without encountering

28

problems, even go nude. He wouldn't go *that* far, of course. But it would add to the thrill, the sense of control, if his garb were something unusual, daring, an implied challenge to the normal world. Thus came to mind the loincloth. He shopped for it online, chose leopard over zebra pattern, had it shipped to his private mailbox.

With Heidi off on errands one Saturday, he stood before a full-length mirror in his new garment. He liked what he saw. Though he didn't work out much, he had a naturally strong-looking build. The effect was diminished by his high brow and glasses, but overall he presented a good closet Tarzan. He couldn't resist striking a few poses.

The first night he wore it he did not venture far. His neighbors to either side were of little interest, so he softly strode to the distant rear boundary of his lot, stood among trees and bushes facing the property behind. Across their backyard, in a lighted upstairs window, a high school girl was wont to change her clothes and do exercises in a topless state. He watched now as she prepared for bed, exercise apparently over. He reflected on a discovery he'd made long before: many young women off the ground floor will not bother to cover their windows when they undress. As if no one might be looking up from a distance, or peering at them through binoculars from an upstairs bathroom across the yards. Which Arnold did, of course.

The girl's light went out and he ducked into the foliage. He considered which direction to take along the property lines. To the north he'd come to an eyesore of a house with a worse eyesore of a garage, an embarrassment to the neighborhood. An old man lived there, often doing something with power tools in the garage. Arnold had never spoken with him but enjoyed snooping there, seeing what the old man was up to, whether he was sober or drunk, alive or dead. But then there were the feral cats who lived in a refuse pile there, a legacy of the man's late wife. They might not react calmly to the leopard skin, sometimes were nasty, did things as a pack. Arnold decided he'd prowl to the south instead.

He passed along the quiet yards, occasionally disturbing small animals, hearing the song of insects, night birds, frogs of some sort. At the end of his block was a rustic-looking house with wagon wheels and such decorating the yard. Arnold had noticed numerous men, restless and confused in appearance, living here for brief periods. They would often be seated at a picnic table beneath a huge oak tree, having animated discussions. It was apparently a "halfway house" of some sort. No one was out just now, though, so Arnold could trot across the adjacent road with easy secrecy. Anyone spotting him from afar would assume he was one of the drifters.

He crossed diagonally across an expansive church property. Across the lawns and parking lots he saw a light burning in the 24-hour chapel, which was a wing of the main church. There would be one or two worshipers in it, since it was always supposed to be manned, but he'd like to enter it some night. He envisioned himself on the cross, hanging there in his loincloth, caressed by the gentle holy lights. Perhaps on a night when no one showed up, with a mask of some sort just in case. To be seen but not identified was okay. It might even enhance his enjoyment, his sense of power without accountability. But this was just his first night in the loincloth. He mustn't go too far.

He passed from the church property to the grounds of a religious high school. He wouldn't visit the school itself, which was likely full of security devices, but instead approached the "brothers' residence," where several religious faculty members lived. It was a simple one-story structure, and he saw that two of the four men were still up. One was the principal, whom Arnold had spotted in a local casino and dubbed Brother Ace. The other was an aloof, studious man he thought of as Brother Hubert. Having retired for the night, apparently, were Brother Tuck, a heavy eater, and Brother Ichabod, who seemed the oldest but dragged himself through long distance runs in all weather. Arnold decided to avoid Brother Ace but to spy a bit on Brother Hubert, who was several rooms away.

He crouched on the ground facing Hubert's window, which was on a corner of the building nearest the school. Through partially closed blinds flashed multicolored light from a television screen. Arnold discerned a profile of the brother's face, rapt in the illumination. Perhaps he was watching porn, Arnold considered. He found a small stone in the grass and sent it in a high, soft arc toward Hubert's window. It glanced off with a nice click, anomalous in the quiet suburban night. The brother reacted quickly, coming to the window and peeking through the blinds, then raising them for a panoramic view. But Arnold was lying face-down, invisible in the darkness. As Hubert turned away to extinguish his light, the man in the loincloth slipped away, leaving only pure darkness for the view from the window.

He felt quite a lift at work the next day. Not only was life balanced by his nightly excursions, but he'd actually gained an edge on it now, on those scrutinizers who'd tormented him. The leopard-skin loincloth gave him an identity–additional to the activity–that his adversaries knew nothing about. What they scrutinized was meaningless now since his real life, his real self, lay in the night. They noticed his new lightness of manner, adding notes of collegiality to the respect owed his knowledge of finance. Even on the commuter train, where he'd ridden as an anonymous stiff, he now felt on a par with the men who exuded prosperity. He could match their ease of manner and relate with them. He even decided to pick up a roll of quarters so he could flip them to the panhandlers.

In the ensuing nights he steadily expanded his roaming range. He crossed streets at the dark spots, where lighting was weakest, and kept as much as possible to the rear property lines. He'd always carried treats for any dogs left out at night, but to these he now added pepper spray. The loincloth required more insurance against discovery. At some point, of course, he might *want* to be seen, to exhibit his persona, but it had to be planned and yield no clue to his daylight identity. Friday and Saturday nights he stayed home, Heidi staying up later since she wasn't rising early for work. Arnold didn't mind since it made his rounds all the sweeter when he resumed them.

"You've been rather chipper lately," she said.

"Have I?"

"Yes. Good news at the firm?"

"Nothing that matters financially. Minor staff changes. More tolerable group now."

They were having tuna casserole, his favorite among Heidi's entrees.

"You know, Arnold, I appreciate your adjustment. And I'm impressed by it."

"The night schedule, you mean?"

"Yes. You don't get too bored, do you? Or lonely? You find enough to do?"

He shrugged.

"Always something doing on the Internet."

"Like what, for instance?"

She always had to complicate things, he thought, couldn't leave well enough alone.

"Oh," he replied, "the *Journal*, online edition."

"But don't you read it on the train?"

"Well, I've been talking more with my fellow passengers. Getting sociable. Part of feeling chipper, I guess."

"Oh, that's nice. That's *great*, Arnold!"

Actually, he'd been catching up on his sleep when he commuted. While he was disciplined in his forays, they often took him past a normal bedtime. Heidi, a deep sleeper, was none the wiser, but a second life simply had to impact his first one. Rather than having oodles of time to read business news, he now had none. But he need not read the *Journal* to do his work, he thought, for he now relied mostly on instinct, anyway. This was consistent with his life and attitude in the leopard-skin loincloth.

One night he ventured beyond the brothers' residence and their academy to the spacious grounds of the local public high school. The large building on the far end had security lighting, but the long stretch of athletic fields did not. Arnold could walk freely in the open, inhale the night's fragrance, listen to night sounds near and far. He tested a rubberized running track, stood atop a pitcher's mound with arms akimbo. King of the hill, he reflected. As he was moving on, however, toward the enclosed football field with its bleachers, he thought he heard a voice or two in the distance, and a giggle. Had he been seen? He crouched low and searched the night in all directions. When again he heard a voice–a girl's–he focused on its direction and spotted an anomaly in the shadows beneath the bleachers. There were people on the ground–a couple and two or three others more distant–occupied with each other and smoking. He had not been seen. He felt relief, but resolved to be more careful in the future. To be scrutinized in this second life would defeat its essential purpose.

Heidi had little awareness of his sensitivity to attention. She took their marriage for granted, as being without issues, which freed her to do as she wished. This was why Arnold had married her, to balance and assuage his life under a micromanaging mother. He'd been her firstborn, suffering her constant corrections while his younger brother went scot-free. Their folksy father could not correct the situation. But now, with Heidi, Arnold had a buffer against all that. She was plain and rather bony, inclined to speak in a monotone, but he'd accepted her as the best of his possible matches in a world of unwelcome people.

There was a man on the train, Alec, who'd taken some advantage of Arnold's lighter manner. The catch-up nap could be disrupted by Alec's litany of complaints: about his job, his family, and modern society. Disturbed in this way one morning, Arnold was inspired to respond frankly from his new perspective, to proselytize.

"Maybe you need another life," he said.

"Another life?"

"Yes. Something completely separate from what you've got now."

Alec gave him a puzzled look.

"You mean just take off? Ditch it all and start over?"

"No, you keep it all, or most of it. But you add something, a nice pleasant routine, probably in secret. A private second life."

The other man stared into space, considering. His stunned conventional features, Arnold thought, bespoke the ignorance of middle-class working men. They had been brainwashed by their culture.

"What *kind* of second life?" Alec asked.

"That's up to you. Could be anything, just so it's sustainable and you enjoy it."

"We're not talking mistress here, are we?" A wink. "Or is it just a secret fishing hole?"

"It *is* best to keep things simple. After all, it has to fit in with your usual life, and secretly." Arnold paused, making a decision. "Let me tell you about a guy I met, one who did what I'm talking about. He started with just a walk."

"A walk?"

"One that became very special, evolved."

He related his own history of late-night perambulation, converting to third person and omitting identifying details. He tried to affect a monotone, not show how much he relished some parts, hoping his eyes or body language didn't betray him. But he soon saw that he needn't be concerned. Alec tended to look away as if trying to picture things, smiling in the comfort of vicarious enjoyment.

"That's some yarn," he commented. "You believe the guy?"

Arnold shrugged.

"He seemed candid enough. Of course, I don't know him well."

Alec looked away again.

"I don't know. All that seems sort of—well, extreme. I mean, I can see what you're talking about, the carving out personal space and all. But I don't want to get branded a nut. Secrets get found out, after all. Then what do you do?"

Arnold didn't hazard an answer. For himself, the possibility was part of the thrill, and he felt confident he could keep it from happening. But his seatmate wasn't cut from the same cloth as he, could never be as daring or resourceful. And neither could the other men on this train. This reinforced for Arnold the specialness, the exclusivity, of the persona he'd created for himself. He was one of a kind, or at least a rare breed.

Most people, he saw, could not even appreciate what he'd accomplished. They'd consider him a "nut," as Alec had implied. Nonetheless, Arnold felt an urge to display his second self, to have its existence affirmed by being witnessed. He'd abandoned one such plan, the hanging on the cross in the 24-hour chapel. The indoor exposure was too risky; the lighting and hindered escape would endanger his first identity. What he desired was a sort of flash appearance, like the split-second scenes in movie and TV previews. He'd expanded his roaming to several blocks in each direction, so he would choose the best spot within that radius.

To the west of the high schools and somewhat north, beyond another zone of housing, lay a large public park. It was bounded on two sides by major streets. Arnold approached along rear property lines, as usual, but also felt safe on the narrow, shaded side streets. The park itself was a sudden change. Unlike the high school grounds, there were lights on tall poles over the whole space. Arnold hesitated on the fringe, still among bushes, and surveyed the scene. Traffic was light at this hour on the intersecting streets, but there were cars in the parking lot. He saw two people on the grass in the center of the park, another couple to the north, someone walking a dog along the street to the west, and a man drinking behind the park building. Arnold snapped clip-on sunglasses over his horn-rims, took a breath, and trotted lightly into the open parkland.

Keeping to the east side of the park, he passed the young man and woman in its center. She seemed to not notice him while her boyfriend stared blankly. Arnold passed in and out of the high lighting, trying to sustain his faun-like trot, avoid a sprint or desultory jog. As he approached the north end of the park, he could see he'd been noticed there by the second couple. They'd looked up from their tete-a-tete and the man was grinning in amusement. Arnold turned toward the west before he reached them.

"Aw, c'mon," he heard the man say.

Arnold concentrated on his pace, on his feet in the grass.

"Hey, fairy!" the man shouted behind him.

Arnold inwardly flinched.

"Fairy!" came the voice once more.

The western side of the park was near, the dog-walker discreetly glancing over, his dog uninterested. Arnold made the turn to trot south, scanning the car traffic for reactions. There were none. He was a lone, graceful runner, his second self asserting its viability. He clung to his pride in this, telling himself that the shouter had just been an idiot. The flicker of irritation would soon pass. Yet he wasn't quite focused as he approached the southern park area, the building and the parking lot beyond. The drinking man had been sitting but was now standing, staring fixedly at this man in leopard-skin and sunglasses. Arnold made his turn to the east and heard some bitter grumbling, fortunately unintelligible. The sentiment was clear, however, piercing the night like a growl from a lower animal. He should dismiss it as such, Arnold knew, but it served to reinforce the pejorative from before, with the evident consensus on him one of disgust.

He entered some bushes on the eastern fringe of the park, feeling relief above all else.

He tried to smile on the dark trek home, take pride again in his foray, but his thoughts became confused. Had there been signs from others despite his secrecy? Alec on the train had not been seeking him out lately, ever since Arnold's story of "a guy's" second life. The other regulars in the car had also become distant toward him. People at the office had seemed friendly enough, but were they patronizing him? Even Heidi he couldn't be sure of. *Especially* Heidi, who had the most opportunity to scrutinize him. But he mustn't get carried away, Arnold knew. A gate had been opened to self-doubt, but it needn't become a floodgate. He had to stay in control.

The next day he was cautious toward people, cool in manner, no longer interested in their fellowship or acceptance. With Heidi he tried to relax, appear normal, but he was still wary. Her early-to-bed routine was especially welcome. Left on his own, Arnold had a mental picture of his leopard-skin loincloth, folded into its hiding place among the heating and cooling ducts in the utility room. It would have to remain there this night, no matter his frustration. Risk management required a night of abstention.

Needing an alternate diversion, Arnold dismissed the television as too passive. Likewise reading the *Journal*, though he'd anyhow stopped relying on it. He sat at the computer and logged on to the Internet, where something was always doing per his assurance to Heidi. But he found that shocks and celebrities, and what passed for interaction, were woefully inferior to his physical transport through the night. Virtual reality lacked virtue. Restless, he surfed without purpose until he recalled the high school girl in the house to the rear. He logged off.

Bathroom door locked, lights off, Arnold stepped into the

dry bathtub and cranked open the small vent window. He raised his powerful binoculars and adjusted the focus. There she was. A slow smile crossed his face as he viewed her crossings of the room, her holding up garments against her body as she posed before a mirror. The only garment she actually wore was a pair of red panties. *Shiny* red, Arnold observed, with a lacy fringe of some sort. He hadn't seen those before. The girl also posed without holding the garments, viewing her trim young body in profile. And she did exercises. Arnold's favorite was when she faced the window and swung a pair of bowling pins at her sides, raising knees high as she marched in place. He felt intimate with her then, her magnified image directly facing him, both she and he smiling joyfully.

After a time the girl slipped downward, out of Arnold's sight, for some activity on the floor. He'd sometimes watch until she went to bed, but these drop-downs could last a long time so he often quit on them. This would be one of those nights, he decided. He cranked shut the vent window and retreated from the bathtub. He felt a residual pleasure, though not of course the catharsis of his prowls.

The following day was a Thursday. Arnold passed the workday feeling hollow, missing the rejuvenation he'd come to expect for his days at the office. The coming night would be his last chance that week to experience his second life. He had to make it count. It suddenly occurred to him, on this score, that he might be developing a dependency. The walks as they progressed had seemed a wonderful addition to his existence, another dimension. But he wondered whether, rather than being a pure supplement, his loincloth life was filling a void, some deficiency in his character or personality. He might have been aware of it at some level, felt a need. His secret life would not then be an enhancement, but a cover for a defect. And yet, from the beginning, he'd felt drawn to it instinctively. Whatever self-knowledge existed in some remote portion of his brain, whatever level of dependency there was, he had to trust in his instinct. It wasn't perfect but it had served pretty well and was his surest guide for now. The long run could be faced later.

That night, Arnold's resolve was firm as he donned the loincloth in his downstairs utility room. He felt strong as he ascended the dark stairwell outside. As he crossed the backyard, however, the late-hour air was somehow less familiar to him. It seemed his absence of the night before had loosened his control of the night, opened it to new possibilities. He stood at the property line with less than his usual confidence. He'd compromise this night, he thought. He'd modify his prowl to observe the closer limits he'd had before. Perhaps another visit to the brothers, a check on Brother Hubert with his porn shows. But no, that wouldn't be enough. Too tame and repetitious. Now, Brother Ace would be a different story. Poring over his racing forms for the next day, maybe on the phone with Vegas or his bookie, or absorbed in an online poker game. But how would Ace react if he saw Arnold peeking in? Not with Brother Hubert's gentility. There was money at stake, after all, and he might well have a gun.

Arnold decided to take the opposite direction, visit the hovel of the old man with its colony of feral cats. As he passed between the yards he felt curiously out of place, familiar with all he saw and yet foreign to it, until he questioned his own feelings, their relevance and even their reality. Had the value of his secret life depended upon illusion? He steadied himself, concentrating on the grass beneath his feet, which grew sparse at the edge of the old man's yard. Ahead was the shadowy refuse heap, two or three pairs of eyes glowing from it. Arnold slowed and stopped. There was movement toward the rear of the heap and he sensed four of them now, perhaps five. He felt that he'd come, unexpectedly but not tragically, to a fateful moment, a time of decision. Yet he was still unthinking, still trusting to instinct. He removed the small carry-pouch from his waist, gripped the top edge of his loincloth, and lowered it past his knees. He stepped out of it. He held the garment tentatively a moment, then flung it in a soft arc onto the refuse heap. The front cat flinched but none immediately moved. Arnold was gone before they could feel threatened.

He returned to the house with more than his usual stealth. A tinge of embarrassment struck as he crossed his backyard to the dark stairwell. It was clearly over, he realized. After dressing he made himself a drink and sat in the large den next to the utility room. Though the house was a split-level, the sleeping Heidi lay directly above, one full story up. Arnold felt an urge to join her, to put this night–all these nights–behind him. But he had to hold off, he knew, and be there at the expected time. There must be nothing unusual to arouse attention. One thing could lead to another until it all came out. He must be guided now by his intellect.

The weekend came as a welcome respite, rather than the interruption it had lately been. He was solicitous toward Heidi, complimenting her mushroom souffle and sitting without complaint through a corny movie she selected. On Sunday she brought him to the herbarium and he easily feigned interest. There was a trendy restaurant in the arboretum proper, its windows overlooking the lagoon and surrounding plant collections, trees filling the middle distance. They sat across from each other with the view of manicured nature beside them.

"We should do this more often," Heidi said, "or things like it."

"Yes," Arnold agreed, "we should."

"How did we get away from it, anyway? The little plays, the music, the drives up north. The wondrous life."

Time went by, Arnold thought as he hesitated. We're not the same people. But that wouldn't do for an answer.

"There was work," he said. "Relatives. Projects at home."

But that didn't seem to do, either. She was looking out over the lagoon, her face still, thoughts perhaps drifting into useless, dangerous territory. Why should there only be the two of them? Why hadn't they tried again after their catastrophe?

"Anyway," he said, "we're here now. This beautiful setting."

"Yes," Heidi answered, "here we are."

Arnold resumed his habit of picking up the *Journal* and reading it on the train. At the office he became again the bland master of finance, neither gregarious nor aloof. In the late evenings he gravitated to the home computer. He knew this was a banal response to things, at some level not respecting himself for it, but it was a safe alternative to the reckless old forays. It was a necessary haven, which was something his life in general now required: a rock-hard shell of protection.

He'd lived with this resolve for several days when he received a package in his office at work. It was in a postal service box and had been sent by overnight mail. The postmark was from the suburb in which he lived, but–even more oddly–the return address was his own, minus the name. Arnold examined the box and shook it but could determine nothing. At length he opened it.

The contents were cushioned and covered by tissue paper, as if they were a heartfelt gift. Spreading the tissue aside, Arnold saw his leopard-skin loincloth, neatly folded. The cats had done little or no damage. A small note, folded once, was pinned to the loincloth, the word "You" inscribed on the visible side. It was in a delicate, unfamiliar hand. Arnold unpinned the note and opened it.

"Tonight," it read. "The back yard border." An apparent signature: "Your Performer," followed by "P.S.–Don't throw these away."

Within the tempest, Arnold remained calm, concentrating. His *performer*, as he'd become hers. His picture on her "smart phone," probably. His work address via the Internet, using his name from public property records. Or maybe Heidi blabbed to the parents. But why did the girl say "these?" Why use that word? And no mention of money, so what did she want? Maybe there was another note–

He picked up the leopard-skin loincloth, letting the folds fall out, and with them a pair of shiny red panties, frilled along the edges.

Arnold sat stunned a moment, then hastily concealed the garments.

STAYING FOR TEA

Dawn broke over the small city, its rosy light gentle on the square roofs of Terence's neighborhood, his bedroom window, the spread on his wife's unoccupied bed. He viewed it while lying on his side, waking, an ache stirring within him. Beatrice was gone for a few days, visiting her family in a larger city, helping with issues. Terence accepted this—her being gone—and she was free to go whenever she wished as far as he was concerned, even though he wanted her. This was because he knew she'd be back soon and anyway he had his work, which was what mattered most to him.

He got up and knocked off his exercises, sit-ups and some stretching, then started some coffee in the kitchen. He dressed while it was brewing: shiny shoes and pants with a crease, clean shirt and that archaic symbol, the tie. He'd leave the knot loose until he approached his work building, as usual. Back in the kitchen, he nibbled on a protein-and-fiber bar with his coffee. Beatrice would insist on making him breakfast if she were there, and he'd accept it, enjoy it. But he truly believed in only one real meal, that being dinner, and so was on the lean side. He had a hungry look, some people thought, but it wasn't hunger for food.

Having bathed and shaved the evening before, Terence needed only to brush his hair and be on his way. The hair was a murky brown that Terence disliked, and it could be unruly. He was looking forward to gaining some gray in it, which he thought would lend him some dignity, a mature look that would lead others to have confidence in him. He never mentioned this to Beatrice, of course. It was a work thing.

Leaving the house, Terence unplugged his car from the recharge pillar and hummed off down the street. No one else was visible except, of course, the sentry in his kiosk on the corner. Terence always got a salute from this man, who knew from his book that Terence was a colleague. There was a reverse reaction from the neighbors, unfortunately. Their misguided fears of the system made them leerier of Terence than they were of the sentries, whose duties were much simpler. The sentries were at two-block intervals here, less frequent than the denser neighborhoods. Out in the country they sat in watch towers.

Terence drove to the outskirts of town and beyond, to a gray stone complex set within played-out farmland. There was a large office building adjacent to a walled area with prison buildings inside. About a quarter-mile down the road was a cluster of small businesses that catered to employees of the complex and visitors. A curving drive led to the facility's parking lots, passing a massive upright slab with thick bronze lettering: *DSI*. Smaller letters in black explained the acronym: *Department of Social Integrity*, and gave mundane details.

He passed through medium security—guards in the lobby, cameras by the elevators, keypads at his floor—and strode to his desk in a large open office area. Few others had arrived, just a couple at a distance and evidently John, the manager, whose cubicle door was open. There were a few phone messages, one annoyingly stuck to the top edge of his monitor. There were several papers in the *IN* box, as well as a thin folder, no doubt a new case assigned to him by John. Terence fished it out, ignoring the other papers and whatever was on the computer.

He saw it was a Potential, the higher priority type for most

Justice Workers. There were also Actuals, who'd officially committed offenses, but that work was just held over from the old Probation Officer position. Their offenses were mostly minor since major, violent crimes were now swiftly punished with execution, sometimes brain altering, following expedited trials. It was to prevent things reaching that stage that people identified as potential offenders were assigned to Justice Workers for control. A Potential had a J.W. for life and was constantly monitored, all actions subject to official disapproval.

It was possible to be deemed a Potential in childhood, but only upon failure of corrective punishment, which took various forms and usually resulted from misbehavior in school. Much more common was Potentiality in adolescence, often seen in misplaced aggression, sexual non-control, and stealing. Besides becoming a Potential, the adolescent was disqualified from any professional role in society and could not bear children. Adults could become Potentials by defiance or disrespect of lawful authority, by neglect of work or living standards, or by degrading themselves or others. Everyone knew the penalty was for threatening the quality of society, so most strove to comply with prescribed mores.

This Potential was an adult, female, and lived a great distance from home base. A teacher age 24, she'd gotten into a heated argument with her principal over the punishment of a student. She'd engaged in verbal abuse, profanity, thrown something, though apparently not at the principal. He wanted to fire her and press charges, but was told he could not. She was suspended and deemed a Potential Offender, not mentally defective since she was a teacher. In addition, her Potential status was subject to expungement, a "sponge" in Department lingo. She was getting off easy, Terence saw, and might come away unscathed. His reports would be more important than usual. He should make sure John appreciated that.

"This sponge you dropped on me. It's out of our region."

"I checked with Court Administration. No mistake. They want it here."

Terence nodded. He'd had to go with the obvious first.

"Pretty soft disposition. Family must have connections."

John looked pained.

"You know I have nothing on that. It's just another case to me. Should be for you, too. Stay objective, Terry."

So he doesn't want to talk about it, Terence thought.

"It's an overnighter," he threw out. He could have added that he was married, but John well knew it.

"Put it on your expense account."

"Right. Thanks for your guidance."

※◆┼3◆┊◆£┼◆※

The Potential's house was on a rise well back from the road, separated from its distant neighbors by a mixture of deciduous trees and evergreens. It was approached by a circular drive that branched off to some outbuildings in back. The house itself was a large split-level log cabin, well maintained and suggestive of comfort and prosperity. Parking in front and walking to the door, Terence fought the sense that he was being impudent, imposing on his economic superiors.

A short woman dressed in maid's attire answered the door. Terence introduced himself and gave the purpose of his visit. He was shown to a spacious parlor and asked to wait while the maid went to fetch his client. The house was dead quiet. Terence saw that its log motif extended to the inner walls, on which several rifles were mounted. Through the windows, he noticed, the sky was turning gray. Time passed. When the maid returned, she was alone.

"I'm sorry. Joanna stepped out a little while ago. But I called her just now and she's coming back."

46

"All right. Fine." He smiled to reassure the woman, who withdrew rather flustered.

Time continued to pass. The sky turned a darker gray.

The silence was suddenly broken by a powerful-sounding car coming to a screeching halt in front of the house. One of its doors slammed and Terence heard a hasty approach and entrance by someone in high heels. He braced himself, recalling the incident with the principal. She was quickly before him, towering it seemed, though her slimness exaggerated her height to the sitting Terence. She also had golden-blond hair reaching to her waist, full and swaying with her every movement. She wore a short leather jacket open in front, with a large matching handbag she held by its straps, her car keys still in her other hand.

"Sorry you had to wait."

"That's okay, it wasn't long."

He felt oddly meek before her, as if he were the client. He gave his head a quick shake.

She sat down opposite and became attentive. Her face was lightly tanned, her features in pleasing concordance.

"Much of this has already been explained to you," he said, then explained again her legal situation and his role in it. Even more than was usual with this, he came to feel like a bureaucratic idiot. "So, what's your own take on all this?" he finally asked.

She smiled and he tried to hide his pleasure, his admiration. Outside, there were distant lightning flashes.

"Well, what to say?" she seemed to wonder aloud. "I've been living here with my dad, when he's not away on business, and everything was fine, flowing along smoothly, until—well, the incident." She hesitated, frowning slightly. "I don't know, it wasn't really me, my usual self I mean. I think I wanted to make a point, felt strongly about it, saw I wasn't getting through to him, decided—consciously decided—that I had to do something more, something outside my natural ways. And so it happened, the incident. I know of course I was wrong. I know that *now*, I mean. One has to stay within limits, within herself as a person, within the rules, the laws. Otherwise there will be problems. Always. I see that now, clearly. Very, very clearly."

She was sincere, Terence thought. He might be influenced by her appearance but, without doubt, it served to reinforce her innocence. He saw no need to be skeptical. He moved on to her background information, verifying with her what he'd been given.

"Have you thought about moving back East?" he asked.

"No, not really. I guess it's an option, but I like it out here, the open spaces and all. My dad's been doing well and I want to also. I want to make this latest thing just a bump in the road. I want to fit in out here, contribute."

"Are you all that set on teaching?"

"Well, it's what I got my degree in."

The maid came in and stood demurely at a distance. Joanna turned to her and gave an inquiring smile.

"I've laid the table, miss."

"Shall we have tea?" Joanna asked Terence.

He was taken aback. He was unfamiliar with the practice, yet it somehow fit the situation, the surroundings.

"Well, I—"

"It's raining now, anyway. You don't want to go off in all this."

He wasn't sure he'd finished the interview but, in any case, Joanna was right. Rain was pelting down and it would likely get worse. Driving would be problematic in these parts.

"Thank you," he half-answered.

They rose to follow the maid into the dining room. Terence saw that Joanna was a foot taller than the other woman, who was also slender and had bobbed hair of a dull brown hue. "Dishwater," he'd heard it called.

"Oh!" Joanna exclaimed as they reached the table. "You put out the wine."

"Since there's a visitor," came the soft response.

"Yes, of course." And, turning to Terence: "We have wine at tea-time on special days sometimes. I guess we can call today special, can't we?"

"Sure," he agreed affably, though of course a bit perplexed. He was obviously still on duty. But it was near the end of his work day and a storm was delaying his departure. So no big deal, he supposed, and a way to wrap things up smoothly.

The table held a silver tea set with cups still on the tray, twin plates of cookies and quarter-sandwiches, and the bottle of white wine in a compact ice bucket. The maid poured them each an ample glass, then departed. Joanna took a seat by one of the place settings, Terence then taking the only other. Outside there was thunder.

"Here's to your visit," Joanna toasted.

Terence clinked glasses with her, inwardly feeling awkward but determined not to show it. He wanted to believe he was in control of the situation. At the same time, there was no denying he felt attracted to this woman.

"Do you have a nice office?" she asked.

He described the layout of DSI, the building and his work area, the different staff positions, their links to the court and other law enforcers. He did not mention the tedium, the occasional grinding sense of futility.

"How's your supervisor?"

"Oh, John is fine. A little testy at times, we have our differences. But he's straightforward, candid, always backs me up. We have some solid trust between us."

"He'll accept your recommendation on me?"

She'd asked it teasingly. He wasn't sure what to say.

"I wouldn't worry about that," he managed.

The talk shifted to movies and television. Joanna nibbled at the cookies and quarter-sandwiches. Terence followed suit and found he was quite hungry. Joanna refilled his wine glass as he devoured the victuals. She noticed his appetite.

"Maybe we could get a real meal together."

"Oh, no. This is fine."

She continued talking about her old girlfriends, their foibles and their boyfriends. The storm outside was raging, the wine running low, but Joanna suddenly looked inspired.

"Say! You know what would go great just now? This nice liqueur my dad picked up! A little dessert for us. Let me get it!"

She was quickly up and into a nearby cabinet, bringing out a fancy bottle with something like *Elixir D'Animale* on its label. She tipped the bottle over little blue glasses, replaced the bottle, and brought the glasses to the table.

"Here you are," she said to Terence, handing him his glass, "fortification against the storm."

He sniffed the glass and sipped. The drink was strong and sweet, as expected, with a plum-like flavor, but also with something else, a penetrating aftertaste that caressed the throat and blossomed on its own within the warmth down below. He sipped again. The flowering kick extended through his body, tingling in his arms and legs. He sipped some more, letting it cut the wine fog until it reached and dominated his brain. He tossed the rest down. As it settled he noticed Joanna was talking but he wasn't understanding her.

Her words ran together, overlapping, so he couldn't sort them out to get her meaning. But it didn't matter because he didn't *care* what she was saying, and he had nothing to say himself. He felt numb indifference, which was satisfactory to him—not demanding the effort of thought. He was in fact incapable of it so clouds closed over his consciousness. It diminished to a pinpoint of light in the vast universe, then was gone.

He awoke atop a king-size bed in a dimly lit bedroom. There was apparently a nightlight somewhere, supplementing the glow from a programmable coffeemaker a yard from his face. The time display read 12:03 a.m. The brewing cycle was just ending and its sound and scent must have awakened him, he reasoned. Beyond that he was mystified. What had happened to the situation he'd been handling? He recalled the beautiful woman, their drinking, her talking, then—what? He'd found himself here, a new and much different situation. One he was not handling. And it was late at night, his visit on department business having extended into wildly unprofessional territory.

He sat up, swung his legs off the bed, saw his jacket on the back of a desk chair, his shoes on the floor beneath it. He looked at the coffeemaker, inhaled the inviting scent. There was a clean mug with a deer's head on it. Groggily standing, he poured himself a full portion. Holding it and gingerly sipping, he took stock of the room, its walls hung with scenes of woods and waterways. She'd talked about her father, he mused, this must be his room. It occurred to him that he should get out of it.

He put on his shoes and jacket, thinking of Joanna taking them off. She must be quite strong to have gotten him up the stairway. The petite maid wouldn't have been much help. Nice that they set up the coffeemaker, a classy touch. Where were they now?

He went to the closed door and opened it, stepped into an unlit hallway. A glow from the lower level let him discern some closed doors. One at the end was ajar, a nightlight inside revealing a bathroom. Coffee in hand, Terence quietly moved to the stairway. He descended.

A single lamp softly lit the parlor, where his briefcase lay where he'd left it, apparently undisturbed. The dining room was darkened, but he could see that the table had been cleared. Moonlight from the window showed the storm had abated. He looked in the spacious kitchen, which had a nightlight by the sink. Everything was put away, nobody around. There was also a den or office, dark within, and another bathroom that Terence wanted to use. But the slightest noise would be startling in the stillness of the house, and his stronger urge was to free himself from this situation, which he now clearly saw as compromising.

Returning to the parlor, he sat and examined his briefcase, put his papers in order as if he'd just finished an interview. He continued drinking his coffee, a permissible indulgence on a professional visit. Having allowed a few minutes for someone to come and see him off, he rose and strode directly to the door, took care with the latches and locks, and exited as silently as possible. Close to nine hours had elapsed since his arrival but, as far as Terence was concerned, he'd never left the parlor.

Outside, he entered the low-hanging boughs of a pine tree to answer his bathroom need. He was soon on his way, slowing for puddles on the winding side roads until he reached the highway. He had an odd combination of feelings as he sped past the intermittent watch towers. As a Justice Worker, he was a colleague of the sentries in these towers, with whom he normally felt solidarity. But his current situation, driving here in the middle of the night after sneaking out of Joanna's house, as well as what went before, lent an aura of absurdity to the whole operation. He shouldn't be out here, he thought, wanted to wash his hands of the matter. He decided to stop at a rest area.

Due to the hour, there were few cars in the lot outside the building. The surrounding countryside was an endless inky expanse. The outside guard watched Terence closely until he showed his DSI badge. Inside, there were washrooms to either side, stone benches in the middle, and snack machines and travel info at the back, along with another guard. Terence sat on one of the benches and brought out his laptop.

"Initial contact completed," he emailed John. "Expungement option was wholly appropriate. In fact, I recommend it be expedited. They're great people, much involved in commerce and community structure. Subject only teaches to give more to society. Fully understands error and pledges non-recurrence. Judging from demeanor with me, suggest principal exaggerated incident in question."

He left it at that regarding the case, only adding that he wasn't sleeping well, might not be in till next day. That would give him time to refocus, he thought. He'd been one of John's most consistent workers, a Department fixture. He needed to maintain that trust, a valuable—no, vital—commodity in the climate of state government. It was harder with Beatrice away. He had no emotional outlet. He was vulnerable and doubts built within him as if from chemical reactions. And so, he assumed, things like this past evening could happen, make his life in this society—and the society itself—look like a shaky house of cards.

He needed to get home, to stop thinking this way.

❦❧❖❧❦

By the following week, Beatrice had returned and Terence was almost back to his usual routine. There was some vague, nagging doubt about the nature of his work, and about the social order, but he tried to keep it filed away in a corner of his psyche. His personal test of normalcy became John, the manager's attitude towards him. He therefore continued his verbal jousting with no obvious effort to ingratiate himself. Whatever John thought of him, however, Terence felt foreboding toward the future cases he'd be getting.

"Don't worry," the manager smiled, "it's not a new one." He dropped the thicker-than-usual file on Terence's desk. "Just add your original notes and walk it to Incineration."

Terence picked up the file as John returned to his office. It was Joanna's case. The order for expungement was attached, his recommendation having swiftly quashed the complaint. The computer file would already be gone. He checked his briefcase and desk for any papers he'd retained, then added them to the file to be burnt. He noticed that its extra thickness was caused by a packet of police materials from the initial responders. Terence's curiosity was piqued. He recalled his bemusement on meeting Joanna, his inability to reconcile her friendly nature with behavior reported for her in the incident. Yet here was evidence that it had happened. Without stopping to consider, he opened the police packet and peered inside.

There were pages of scrawled field notes and smudged copies of material he'd already seen. But there was also a thin, stiff envelope with *Do Not Bend—Photos* printed on it. Joanna's name and a number were handwritten along one edge. With some hesitation, not wanting to change his memory of her and yet drawn to finality, Terence pulled the "mug shots" from the envelope. He sat motionless as he viewed them, only his eyes working, swinging back and forth between front and side views. What he'd known as reality had evaporated in an instant.

The expression on the face was surly, angry, and showed the strain of hysteria. Pure hatred welled from the eyes. The face was pale with spent emotion, the hair unkempt and matted along the forehead. But the hair was not long and it was dark in color. Dishwater brown, Terence knew, though the pictures were black and white.

It was the woman he'd known as the little maid.

Carefully, glancing around the open work area, Terence replaced the photos in the envelope, the envelope in the police packet, the packet in the thick file. He gathered the file under his arm as he rose from his chair. John was in his cubicle, occupied with another worker, the door open. Terence moved off in the opposite direction. He used an alternate exit to the hallway, bypassed the elevators, took a little-used stairway to the basement, which contained their facility for destroying records.

He was simply following directions, Terence told himself, John's direct orders. He was in no way at fault on this.

Nobody was at fault.

THE RIVALRIES

Jack stood at the window of his downtown office, peering down through the dark and a thin snowfall. He was expecting his nephew, Carl, for an after-hours confab. The manuscript Carl had left was now fully edited and lay in the middle of Jack's desk. As a literary agent, he normally didn't provide this service, especially for free, but such was the nature of their relationship. Jack also didn't handle technical works—in this case paleontology—but again there was the need for exception. He was doing his best for the young man, though there were still issues to discuss.

"Stop for a drink?" came a voice from the doorway.

Jack half-turned. It was the podiatrist from down the hall.

"Not tonight, Phil. My nephew again." He nodded toward Carl's manuscript.

"Ah, the big project. Well, till tomorrow, then."

They waved each other off and stillness reasserted itself. It had struck Jack many times how so much that seemed urgent during office hours could be easily forgotten at five o'clock. And for whole weekends, with even the TV news mostly hibernating. And yet the importance of things remained, however great humanity's slide into trivia and animal pleasures. Did meaning become less relevant or did it simply not exist?

There was the sound of elevator doors up the hall, the first since Phil had left, followed by Carl's strong strides on the hall carpeting.

"Hi, Uncle Jack."

"Carl, come in. Come in and have a seat."

There was physical similarity between the two men. They both had spare, angular builds, were a bit above average in height, and wore their wiry hair close-cropped. Had Jack's not gone gray, they might be mistaken for brothers.

"That it?" Carl asked.

"Yes, all edited. As far as I could go, anyway."

"As far as you could go?"

"Well, you yourself could make further revisions."

Carl nodded.

"Our analysis is all there. The conclusions are subject to further discovery, of course. But the dig in Montana has yielded all it's going to, I think."

Jack smiled warmly, reassuringly.

"You're the expert."

His nephew gave a modest shrug.

"There's just one thing, Carl, a general sort of thing. Not about the substance of your work. That's all fine as far as I'm concerned. Or about the mechanics or style of your manuscript. That's great, too. It's really just a personal, purely subjective observation."

"Okay," Carl smiled, "let me have it."

"Well, it seems that your discovery—big as it is, monumental—was the outgrowth, in a way, of the earlier project under Professor Morowitz. You wouldn't have been there, after all, if you hadn't worked for him on the dinosaur. Neither would your colleague, Rhea. So, with that and the proximity of your find to the dinosaur dig, I'm wondering if you really want to treat it as separate from the Morowitz project. You might project more candor, more credibility, if the connection were clearly acknowledged."

Carl's upbeat expression had changed to one quite serious.

"Our dig was completely outside the perimeter of Morowitz's. And of course, our find is a much different species."

"Though within the same geological stratum. That's the key to its significance, is it not?"

Carl relaxed and tried a different tack.

"Look, Uncle Jack, Dr. Morowitz wasn't very involved even on the dinosaur dig. He made some initial arrangements, but he wasn't at the site—ever—until the very end, the picture-taking and press release. Yet he took full credit, with the press and in his article, not even mentioning his research assistants. All that hard and meticulous work, then zero acknowledgement. To give him any credit on the new find would be—well, something that shouldn't happen."

Jack had avoided mentioning ethics so far, and now was glad he had. It appeared the actual onus was on Morowitz.

"I've heard of this before, a professor hogging credit for assistants' work, but he didn't even list your name?"

"Right, only his own. And some of his text was directly from my notes, with his data the same as Rhea's tables."

Jack sat back, tried to view things objectively, but his sympathy for his nephew remained undiminished.

"Well, we certainly don't want him pulling *that* crap again. Your manuscript will stand as it is."

Carl brightened, regaining the mood he'd arrived in.

"Thanks, Uncle Jack."

"I'll make some contacts over the next few days. We're still avoiding the professional journals?"

"Yes, they'd be swayed too much by Morowitz. It could all fall apart."

"Okay, we'll stay with a general audience. And now, Mr. Discoverer, what do you say to dinner?"

Carl stiffened a bit.

"Well, you see, Uncle Jack, I'm supposed to see Rhea at

the museum after I leave here. She's been working late on the fossil, getting it ready for exhibit." Then, brightening again: "But say, why don't you come with me? You can see the fossil first-hand and then we can *all* go to dinner."

Jack smiled at his nephew's enthusiasm, reflexively nodded his assent.

"Sounds good. I'll just close things up."

It was only a short taxi ride to the museum. In nicer weather they might have walked, but the cold November gusts were present this night. Jack and Carl hastened up the museum's many steps to an employee entrance near the main doors. Carl was already on his phone to Rhea, who could alert Security to let them in.

"Uncle Jack is with me," the nephew said. "I told him he could see Opaline. The article is good to go."

There was a rattling behind the door and it was opened by a stolid security guard. He gave them a cursory inspection while admitting them. Carl knew his way through the deserted halls, leading Jack to an obscure stairway descending into the bowels of the building. They soon found themselves in a dusty, cavernous space with many crated items stored in rows. Lighting was minimal except for two or three points of late work activity. One of these was the fossil preparation lab, where a woman close to Jack's age was picking at large clam shells with what looked like dental implements. Behind her on other tables were various tools, brushes, and bottles of fluid. There were also washtubs, a small jackhammer, and a sand blaster.

"Suzanne," Carl said, "this is my uncle Jack."

The woman smiled.

"Pleased to meet you," Jack proffered.

Suzanne smiled again, having laid down her work. She was about to speak when Rhea strode in from a room at the rear.

"Jack! Good to see you again."

They'd met a couple of times before, when she was with Carl at family functions. He'd introduced her as a coworker first, then as a friend, perhaps building to something more special. She was a slender young woman with fine, light brown hair, always more or less tense while trying to be friendly, accommodating. She was someone with whom Jack sympathized, wanted to put at ease, but her conversation could be abrupt and hit dead ends. Her nervousness, however, would have little impact on her work in paleontology. It was good she had chosen it as a career, fortunate for her and maybe also for Carl.

"Same here," Jack replied to her greeting.

"Carl says we're fine with the article."

"Yes, ready to market. They might want to crop the photos, but I think we'll get them all in."

"They're germane."

"Yes."

"Probative."

"I suppose."

"Might be one more, the finished mounting. We'll see how it turns out."

"How does Opaline look right now?" Carl asked.

"Coming right along," Rhea smiled at him. Then to Jack: "Want to have a look? Verify her existence?"

"Sure. I'm all agog."

Rhea turned to the rear, exiting briskly with Carl and Jack following her.

"Nice meeting you, Jack!" Suzanne called after them.

Jack looked back and threw her a wave.

"This is a more secure room," Rhea explained as they reached it. "It also gives us more privacy when working on high-profile projects."

"Which ours will soon be," Carl added.

On entering, Jack found the room's walls, especially the corners, to be in near-darkness. The room's single light was shaded and suspended low over the middle of the floor, casting harsh illumination on the work in progress below. It had clearly assumed the form of the fossil described in Carl's article: a near-complete skeleton of a mammalian biped standing about four and a half feet tall.

"Uncle Jack," Carl smiled, "meet Opaline."

She was mounted on a wire frame, standing but hunched forward, arms slightly raised and jaws open to better expose the teeth. The fingers and toes were longer and more uniform than on later humans, the teeth larger but otherwise homologous. An extended tailbone showed that she'd had a visible tail.

"The article goes into brain capacity—" Jack began.

"Yes," Rhea picked up quickly, "measured from all angles. Tedious but necessary. It's proportionately about equal to our own. The shape, too."

"What about the brain's functioning?"

"That can only be inferred."

Jack studied the fossil from various perspectives, Rhea and Carl observing his interest, obviously pleased.

"I can see you put in a lot of work. It's a fantastic restoration. Everyone should agree on that."

"There's still a little to be done," Rhea acknowledged. "A few fractures to strengthen, a final cleaning."

"Well, she looks fine to me. Especially after sixty million years."

"Sixty-five," Carl corrected. "Late Cretaceous period."

"Point taken, professor."

"Not quite there yet, Uncle Jack."

"Well, this'll sure help."

Carl and Rhea exchanged smiles.

"And there's the significance," Jack continued, "as you discuss in the article."

"Yes, it was just before the cataclysm, the extinction of the dinosaurs. So Opaline here saw the last of them as she walked the plains and the forests."

"Amazing."

"Simply science," said Rhea. "But science itself is amazing."

"Yes, and here we are her descendants."

"We'd need to find a link to claim that, Uncle Jack. Opaline and her people might have perished in the cataclysm, along with the dinosaurs. There were other races of people, much more recent, who apparently died out."

They stayed with the fossil a while longer, allowing Jack an extended viewing, until he himself suggested they go to dinner. As Rhea finished up in Opaline's room, Jack waited in front with Carl. Suzanne had apparently left for the day. Jack felt some regret that he'd hardly spoken with her, hoped she hadn't thought him rude. It was important to him that he show refinement in middle age.

"There's just the two of them?" he asked Carl.

"No, there's others during the day. Dave, the head, has an office upstairs. Then there's Johan and an intern, Denise I think her name is."

"Not that big a staff."

"Yeah, they were happy to get Rhea. And she feels secure here, glad to be away from Morowitz."

"Hm. Security is important, all right."

⚔

They had dinner at a downtown restaurant, Jack and Rhea having steak while Carl opted for pasta. They were all quite hungry, but Jack noticed how Rhea attacked her steak with unusual aggressiveness. He guessed it was a carryover from chipping away rock from ancient bones. Tedious, she had said. No doubt there was a mounting need for reward during the countless hours of hard, isolated work. He hoped more than ever that all went well with their project, especially the part he was involved in, Carl's article. It had started as a casual favor, but he now saw it as vitally important for this young couple's future together. He'd have to do all he could to help them succeed.

"He was a perfect ass," Rhea said about Morowitz.

"Some people shouldn't have authority," Jack replied. "But you *were* able to work with him awhile, right?"

"It doesn't show right away. He's nice enough at first, till he gets what he wants from you. Then, bam! You're screwed."

"Neither of you talked to him about it?"

"The journal paper was in proofs already," said Carl. "We first found out when we saw them. We were shocked."

"It seems he could have altered the byline, at least, while checking the proofs."

Carl shrugged.

"We were too much in shock, more from the message behind it than the lack of credit. As if we were peons, pawns, mere tools of a wannabe great man."

"Actually," Rhea said, "I did have it out with him a little."

"Rhea—"

"No, Carl. I want to say this. It was overdue, Jack. It went back to when I was new there. There was unwanted—" She hesitated. "Attention. I didn't know what to do, tried to work while fending him off. I couldn't tell anyone or it'd get back to him. Carl and I hardly knew each other then."

"So, harassment?"

Rhea nodded.

"Anyway, the Montana dig was the last straw. I let him know it. He's got this really scummy side to him, Jack."

She drained her second glass of wine. She'd want another,

Jack sensed, and he'd have to join her. Carl, a light drinker, had stopped after one. Jack saw he was bound to this young couple's wishes, more strongly than he'd been to Carl's alone, for reasons outside his understanding. Affairs of the heart were well in the past for him personally, and the intertwined job challenges were new ground. He'd fallen into routines, mental instruction manuals, but saw that he might have to improvise here. It was a new species of situation.

⊷⊱⊰⊱⊰⊷

When sending out packets to chosen publications, Jack would normally wait at least a week for responses. He was surprised, therefore, when a response came just three days after Carl's article went out. The contact was someone Jack had worked with before, an energetic man who at first sounded enthused to Jack. But then a cautionary tone took hold.

"You're fully confident in the authors, are you? That this is their original work?"

"Of course. They're my nephew and his close friend. He gave it to me to edit, piece by piece."

"Oh? You *are* a dedicated agent."

"Well, bloodlines, you know."

"What about the substance of the piece, this discovery?"

"Straight from his notes, which I've seen, and data collected by Rhea, also seen."

"Hm. Well, I'd better give you a heads-up, Jack. We got a query last week about an article on the same thing. It was sketchy. We figured he was holding back till he got a commitment."

"That was regarding this same discovery?"

"Right. Humanoid in same layer as dinosaur."

"And the author's and discoverer's names?"

"Morowitz on both counts."

64

Jack was silent a moment, processing. His surprise at the news was quickly eclipsed by disgust with Morowitz. What gall! But then, how did the professor even *know* about Opaline?

"Can you hold off responding to the query?" he asked the editor.

"Sure, but I doubt we're the only ones picking up on this."

⊕┤3⊃┆⊃Ӡӄ⊖

Jack was at a loss what to do. He'd made a commitment to Carl and Rhea's success, and they'd made greater commitments, so to allow any interference or bogus claim was unthinkable. But who could have informed Morowitz, inducing him to hijack the discovery? Few people knew about it at all, fewer still with access to Carl's and Rhea's details. He himself, in editing Carl's manuscript, was the priviest to those details, aside from Carl and Rhea. He'd kept the manuscript secure, at least he thought he had, so barring break-ins the information did not come from him. But then, how secure had it really been, even with the door locked? About as much as the medical records down the hall, he decided, those of Phil the podiatrist's patients. He might do well to raise the issue over their evening drinks.

"Security?" Phil reacted when Jack mentioned it later. "I haven't given it much thought lately. Not for a long time, in fact. My well-heeled patients no doubt have their secrets, but those don't go in a podiatric file."

"No, I suppose not."

"Why? Something missing from your office?"

"No, not exactly. But something might have been copied, compromised. I got this heads-up on an article I submitted."

"Not your nephew's thing!"

Jack nodded.

65

"Christ, that's bad. Anything family and failed is bad. Ten times the usual effects."

Jack looked at him blankly, no response coming to mind.

"Anyway," Phil went on, "the cleaners don't go into locked offices. Someone must have a key for emergencies, I guess, maybe their supervisor. You can check with the building management."

But Jack now realized that would be useless. He hadn't wanted to admit it to himself, but there was more to this than simple theft or arrogance. There was—there had to be—an element of pernicious deceit. The person or persons who stole the project had to know beforehand how big it was, not only that it existed. They had to have some idea of the details, even while lacking full knowledge, and how it would be of great value to someone like Morowitz, who himself was in the dark. The source of the problem was very close to Carl and Rhea, trusted, an apparent friend who was an agent of disaster.

⊛⟩⊰⊱⟨⊛

Jack was hesitant to inform Carl. He would soon have to, he knew, since the fossil was almost ready for exhibit and publication of the article should be in place. But there was again the family factor, Jack's fear of appearing a failure in his avuncular role. A resolvable question of ethics in professional circles could become The Disaster Involving Jack throughout their family tree. He wanted to avert this, of course, as well as the loss to Carl and Rhea, and thought his best bet was to find and deal with the leaker, and maybe with Morowitz himself. With a little luck he could have the problem in hand before Carl or the relatives even knew about it.

On the morning after he'd consulted Phil, Jack walked briskly through the downtown area to the museum situated on the lakefront. His intention was to drop in on Rhea and inquire about those privy to the discovery. The leaker to Morowitz, after all, was most likely among her coworkers. She and Carl had been assisted in Montana by local students, none of whom were much aware of the details or significance of the find. Carl himself had confided only in Jack.

The museum was open for its normal visitation, though visitors were few since it was a weekday morning. Jack made his way to the fossil preparation lab, where he found Suzanne sitting where he'd last seen her, but apparently alone.

"They're upstairs," she said of her colleagues. "A little maintenance work."

"Rhea, also?"

"No," and she hesitated. "Rhea's been coming later some days, but then she works into evening. Like when you stopped by last week."

"You were here then, too. Makes for a long day."

"Yes," she smiled, "I just about live here."

Jack sat in a chair by Suzanne's work table. She closed a ledger she'd been consulting. She had a fresher look this day, Jack noticed, with her hair in neat little waves. She also wasn't as stout as he'd thought, perhaps owing to the lab coat. She might have been quite attractive when she—when they both—were young. She waited expectantly when he sat down.

"I'd like to ask about something," he said.

"Okay."

"Well, this project, with Opaline, it's supposed to have been secret, right? Until the official announcement?"

"That's the general understanding, yes."

"General. There's not a specific—I mean clearly required—confidentiality?"

"Well, as far as most of the facts go, Rhea keeps them to herself, locked in that room. Dave let her have it when the bones

67

first came in. Dave's our boss. That's why some of this stuff is lying around out here."

She gestured toward the washtubs, small jackhammer, sand blaster. Jack nodded his understanding.

"The reason I ask is, of course, we wouldn't want someone stealing the impact of the announcement, Carl's article, the exhibit itself."

Suzanne stiffened a moment, then relaxed.

"No, of course not." A hesitation. "But even if that were to happen, Jack, the larger cause would still be served, would it not? The cause of science, human knowledge?"

"Perhaps, but not as well. The discovery and hard work of two fine young people would be stolen, at least in part, at least temporarily, while they deserve the entire credit for it."

Suzanne looked down.

"Yes, of course." And, looking up again: "Have you found that someone is trying to interfere?"

"There's been an indication."

Suzanne waited, but Jack wouldn't give details. She finally sighed and moved restlessly in her chair.

"Anyway, as you say, they're both young. They'll come through it all fine. That's more than I can say for some of us."

Jack looked her in the eyes, yielded a smile.

"You've worked here a long time?"

"Eighteen years."

The prime years of your life, Jack thought but didn't say.

"It's been a good career? You've felt appreciated?"

She eyed him warily.

"I'm satisfied for now. But we all have hopes and dreams, don't we? Even you, if I may be so bold. Agenting some big blockbuster, becoming famous—"

She waved in the air toward some fantastic future.

"I suppose," Jack smiled, seeing he was at a dead end.

The conversation soon ended and he left the museum. He

had lingering doubts about Suzanne, despite her smoothness in fending him off. She was closest to Rhea among the staff and had the most opportunity to nose into the project. She was in need of a boost to her career, had little to lose by taking a gamble. He knew from his own quiet hours that, when one is mired in middle age, crazy scenarios can present themselves. Suzanne was familiar with Morowitz, not only his words but, through Rhea, his character. Becoming the man's catalyst to easy glory might seem a lucrative opportunity. With these thoughts in mind as he walked outside, Jack hardly noticed the wind increasing its bite, the sky turning full shale gray.

❄❁❄

Returning to his office building, Jack relaxed as he entered the warmth of the lobby. It must have been comforting for Carl, he thought, coming here to consult an uncle in whom he had full confidence. And it had been easy at first for Jack to justify that confidence, growing closer to his nephew in the process, filling somewhat the gap in his own life. But, as always seemed to happen for Jack, there came unwelcome complications, interference with the simple truths of happiness. He now felt a need to make contact with Carl, give him a call despite the bad situation. He needed to maintain their bond.

Coming to his floor and entering his office, Jack noticed an incoming fax on the machine. He walked over and picked it up. It was a response to one of the packets he'd sent out, an enthusiastic acceptance from a regional monthly magazine, somewhat credulous in its outlook. He'd included them as a safety valve, a last resort in case the others all passed on the science story of the century. They wanted only initial publication rights, for which they offered a modest sum, though no doubt it was all their budget would allow. Jack would normally have filed the offer away for possible but unlikely use later, but this day he kept it in hand. He gazed out his window and reflected. Apparently Morowitz had skipped this one, considered it beneath him probably, yet now it might be the key to his undoing. He, Jack, had the power to immediately accept this offer, locking in publication before Morowitz could complete his own acceptable article. Credit for the discovery and attendant work would be rightfully established for Carl and Rhea.

Without further thought, Jack sat at his desk and signed the acceptance form, then faxed it off with original to be mailed. Strictly speaking, he should have run this by Carl first. But the nephew, having full confidence in Jack, had given his uncle authority to act in his stead. Family ties were again decisive.

Jack turned to his other work, tried to lose himself in it as an escape from Opaline. He no longer felt a pressing need to call Carl since the article had been placed, the Morowitz problem obviated. At lunchtime he stopped by Phil's office, thinking they might step out awhile, but the podiatrist had patients waiting. Jack therefore went by himself into the dark and blustery midday. Ice crystals stung his face as he sought out their favorite haunt. He sat at the bar and had a sandwich with dark beer, as he was wont to do when here for lunch. Then, for no reason he could fathom, he indulged in another frothy pint. He was well into its added comfort when he suddenly felt he'd missed something about the paleontologists. He reviewed all his contacts but saw nothing new. Maybe, he thought, it was simply that he should call Carl after all, share the good news about the placement. It was best to follow up on things, not just let them drop.

Still, on returning again to his office, Jack continued to delay the call. It had occurred to him that Carl would be working at the university, in the paleontology department overseen by Morowitz. It was unclear whether they could talk freely. But, as the afternoon wore on, Jack decided he should call anyway since he might not be able to reach Carl in the evening. They would just have to be guarded in their conversation.

He made the call, was transferred to the department and then to a laboratory. His nephew came on the line.

"Uncle Jack?"

"Hello, Carl."

"This is a surprise. I usually call *you*."

"Yes, well, who's around there, Carl? Do you have some privacy for this?"

"Privacy? Yeah, I guess so. Just an undergrad here with me, doing some grunt work."

"Fine. And this is a secure line, more or less?"

"Yeah, sure. Unless you count the fossils listening." Then, in subdued tone: "What is it, Uncle Jack? Something come up?"

"Actually, yes. It's good news, Carl. The article has been accepted. It'll be published next issue with no strings attached."

"That's great, Uncle Jack. Who accepted it?"

Jack recited the magazine's version of its nature and importance.

"Great," Carl repeated. "Does Rhea know about this?"

"No, not yet. Maybe you can let her know."

"Sure, I'll do that." A pause. "I'm not sure when, though. She'll be working late tonight, catching up on stuff she let slide to work on Opaline. Maybe I'll just call her there."

"Better ask her to keep it private for now, Carl. Even from Suzanne. And make sure no one's listening."

"Okay. But why so much secrecy, Uncle Jack? Aren't we home-free now?"

"We just don't want anything going wrong. Not after your other time."

"Hm, yeah. Guess you're right."

It occurred to Jack that Carl's tone had changed since Rhea was mentioned, become more tentative.

"Everything okay with Rhea?" he asked, meaning "with you two?"

"Oh sure, she's fine. Just a little behind in her work. She's like that, you know? All of a sudden has to clear something up, all at once. Gives it all she's got for a while. That's just her. That's Rhea."

Jack wouldn't say it to his nephew, but he'd often heard this fallacy before. A questionable behavior or attribute would be dismissed with "that's just so-and-so," a useless truism applicable to any weakness or fault, even the more serious. Jack felt renewed concern for his nephew.

"Well, give her my best, then," he said.

"I will, Uncle Jack."

"And I'm still ready to help any way I can. I'm not ducking out just because the article is placed."

"Okay, great. Maybe we can get together later in the week. With Rhea. Celebrate."

"Fine. I'd like that, Carl. Well, take care of yourself."

"You too, Uncle Jack."

They'd finished on a high note, perhaps with some effort. There followed that profound silence that can greet one after a phone conversation. In it Jack realized his love for Carl as a surrogate son, his regard for Rhea as intrinsic to Carl's happiness, and the vulnerability of both of them. Jack knew from his own youth the delicate web of decisions and actions in which futures could be shattered by a single wrong move or an illusion. He'd never challenge Carl's optimism; it was essential for the young. But he hoped more than believed that it was justified.

＊＊＊

Returning to his other work after talking with Carl, Jack found himself unable to focus. He decided that he might as well call it a day. Locking his door, he glanced down the hall toward Phil's office but realized Phil would still be busy. Jack would have to drink alone tonight. On reaching the street, he saw that the snow showed signs of accumulating. The wind had abated somewhat but it was now colder. Yet he felt like walking a bit, relaxing his mind, so he hunched against the elements and set off through the streets.

He was feeling the storm's full sting by the time he reached the side street that contained his hideaway. It was a small but expensive restaurant that he favored for its quiet and unhurried atmosphere. One could drink and dine alone here and not feel in the least awkward. He was shown to a table by the window, ordered a cocktail, then chose steamed whitefish since it took a long time to prepare. He could drink in peace.

Contemplating the street beyond the window, sipping his whiskey, Jack felt the chill leave his body. His mind was again free to function. How, he asked himself, had he arrived here? Sitting alone in this place, a nephew the one closest to him, unseen obstacles still blocking him, blocking his efforts to help. Early on, Jack recalled, there were the blunders in changing jobs, the innocent but critical mistakes in relationships. No way to make those up. Baggage accumulates. You tend to settle for less and less. If you try to hook up with someone your age, they have baggage too. It doesn't really work. You're stuck sitting here by yourself, so many wrong turns it could only end this way. My fate. Settle for the scraps.

The whitefish was served on a covered metal dish with a little cup of caviar in the middle. Jack smiled, at the irony he could appreciate professionally but also at the rebuke. Bring on the rebukes, he thought. At least they're stimulating.

Finishing his meal, he decided to take a cab to his apartment, located in a high-rise north of downtown. A part of him still felt like walking, but the rest of him was wary of the rising snow and the drinks he felt. As it turned out, the snow had congested traffic and the cab moved at a crawl. Jack watched the rush of pedestrians from his cozy back seat. If only it was thinking that accomplished things, he thought, he had so much time for it. But you were always held back by your limitations, and those of other people, so it usually came down to luck or a fix of some sort. Unless you had no scruples or were willing to ditch them awhile, which really meant for good. He detested the idea but understood how it happened. Greed and deceit grew wild in human nature, as did desperation.

He found himself at the high-rise, settled with his driver, elevated to his floor. For one who favored culture, pursuit of higher truths, he often lapsed into mechanical modes of living. But routine can be constructive, he'd tell himself, have a purpose. And anyway, that's just me. This last thought occurred as he flopped face-first on his bed, fully clothed, the fatigue of the day claiming him and blanking his consciousness.

✻⊱❊⊰✻

Jack got up once during the night, a new habit that was taking root. He'd make a bathroom stop, take a small drink of water, and return to bed. Tonight he also glanced out a window to check on the snowfall. It had stopped but had been substantial, illuminated now by bluish light from a quarter moon. Otherworldly, he thought, but thought no further since he needed to take off clothes. He was soon back in his nightly nest, sleep reclaimed.

He awoke as usual to the early news summary on public radio. There were reports on political squabbles, on conflicts across the world, but then on something more immediate, close to home. Very close. City police were at the scene of an apparent homicide that had occurred in the late night or early morning hours. The scene was the museum of natural history

CRISIS ON A COUNTRY ROAD

It was jumbled in Norm's memory, but it must have started with that sign along the highway, one of those mini-billboards announcing amenities at the next exit. There were eight or ten spaces for business names with logos, but only three were filled. He'd been hungry awhile and so noted the only restaurant: Chun Ling's. Odd, he thought, a Chinese place way out here, but it might be a pleasant break from the usual sandwich.

At the base of the exit ramp, across the road that passed under the highway, he found a small strip mall. Three of the four storefronts were vacant, only a small antiques store still active. A gravel road next to the mall ran parallel to the highway. Norm observed a homemade sign: *Chun Ling's Straight Ahead*, and crossed the two-lane blacktop onto the gravel.

The restaurant was about a quarter-mile down, a low dingy building with a mobile home in back. There were no adjoining neighbors, neglected farmland behind, non-descript trees across the gravel road, veiling the highway. Norm parked in a widening of the gravel that he assumed was the parking lot. On entering the building, he found disconcerting dimness, the only light coming from the overcast sky outside. But then he saw he was being watched by the most attractive woman he'd ever seen.

"Please sit where you wish," she said.

He chose a window table. There were no other diners, no

sign of anyone except his hostess. She brought him a one-page menu covered in plastic.

"Sorry, no shrimp today."

There were only ten choices listed, several now eliminated by the lack of shrimp. They did have beer and wine, however. There were three domestic beers and one import, with the wines listed simply as red, white, and plum.

"I'll go with the chicken and mixed vegetables, and I guess a Tsingtao."

"Excellent."

She moved soundlessly away, cascading black hair distinct on white dress, then fading in the shadows of the room. Norm turned his gaze to the window, the motionless outdoors. No one passed on the gravel road. There were small noises, eventually, from the kitchen, and he wondered if she was cooking his meal herself. But the noises continued as she brought beer and an egg roll to his table.

"About five minutes," she said.

"Okay, fine."

It was like many of his situations, Norm thought. He'd meet someone out of the blue, without warning, and he'd be unable to relate because it was *too much* out of the blue—he knew nothing about her. He was stuck with standard responses, mechanical stuff, then later felt he'd failed. This time could be worse than usual since he found her so beautiful.

The food came.

"The plate is hot," she warned. "Will you want more beer?"

"No, this is fine."

She moved away. As Norm picked up his fork, he noticed her stopping at the entrance door, bringing out a bulky key ring, locking the restaurant up. An *Open* sign was reversed to *Closed*.

"Last customer," she smiled. "I will let you out."

Norm glanced at his watch, saw it was 4:20 p.m. Odd time to be closing, he thought, but then he was drawn to his meal. The food was rather bland but he was hungry and so was satisfied. The sounds of his eating and pouring beer were the only ones in the room. Without them, utter stillness. His hostess appeared promptly as he finished, check in hand.

"I hope you enjoyed. Please pay at the register."

"Sure."

He followed directions, winding past empty tables and paying in cash so he could tell her to keep the change. For this he received another smile. Successful stop, he thought. As good as he could do, anyway.

He left and she re-locked the door behind him.

Clouds of dust rose as he backed his car and swung around to return to the highway. Emerging from the dust, he saw another car parked a short way up the road. It crouched under ragged trees, two or more people within, staring in the direction of the restaurant. Norm gave them a fleeting glance as he passed. Two men in front: the driver light-complected, the passenger dark. A smaller man in back, Asian cast, leaning forward between the others. Norm continued down the gravel road to the two-lane blacktop, turned left toward the entrance ramp, but slowed and pulled off before he reached it.

He was bothered: multi-racial trio lurking, isolated business closing, beautiful woman inside. No way he could leave her there. Not while he was bothered.

He made a smooth U-turn, drove into the mini-mall, parked at the end away from the gravel road. He was before one of the vacant storefronts, the antiques place being at the other end. If anyone asked, he could be a prospective renter. They wouldn't know he was carrying the gun he was now taking from under his seat.

Outside, he peered into the vacant storefront as if inspecting it, then slipped around the side of the building. The rear of the mall gave way to a tangle of rough growth that Norm entered to return to the restaurant. The footing became easier and he was soon at the point where he'd seen the other car, but it was gone. He spotted it in front of the restaurant, parked parallel to the entrance door, the smaller man standing by the car and then getting in behind the wheel. The other two were apparently in the restaurant. Norm edged toward the near side of the building, hoping to spy through the windows. He hadn't quite reached it when there was rapid movement within: his hostess, being muscled through the dining room and out the door by the light-complected man.

Norm's first instinct was to follow, gun in hand, and gain an advantage by the car. But there was still the dark man. The advantage might quickly be reversed. So Norm sidled along the wall to a window opening to the kitchen, peeked in a lower corner, saw a middle-aged cook removing documents from a box while a gun was trained on him. The gunman was turned away from the window, watching the cook closely, leaving Norm an easy shot through the glass. Norm took it, calmly but without hesitation, unthinking.

The hesitation came a moment later, with the man down and the cook in suspended animation. Norm didn't know what to shout, could only signal toward the front and show alliance.

"I'm going up there!" he called through broken glass.

He'd hardly moved, however, before the cook himself scooped up the gun on the floor and ran into the dining room. Norm advanced along the outside wall. Two shots rang out before he reached the corner of the building. He stopped and heard shouts in Chinese, apparently the cook. Norm peered around the corner and saw the lighter man sprawled in the gravel, the woman in the car, the cook advancing with pistol raised. Just then the car's motor was gunned and it threw up gravel as the smaller man tried to flee. Norm ran up to join the cook, who was aiming his weapon at the car.

"Aim low and get tires!" he yelled at Norm.

So they stood together in the gravel and billowing dust,

firing guns at the departing car, which was slowed by lack of traction. The driver still floored the gas pedal. He succeeded when the right wheels left the road, but very suddenly so that he lost control. The car swerved sharply to the left and went off the road on the highway side. It shot over packed earth, clearing the trees, then slammed into a concrete highway abutment. Almost instantly it exploded.

Norm stood in shock, the cook venting his anguish in Chinese. He was still shouting as he moved to approach the flaming wreck.

"I'll get help!" Norm called after him, and hastened back toward the restaurant.

As he viewed the assailant lying in the gravel, however, and envisioned the one inside, Norm felt revulsion toward the whole situation. There was also fear: of being sucked in more, of being ruined. He therefore trotted past and around the building into the nondescript stretch he had crossed from the mini-mall. He'd make the call from his cell phone, which was in the car. He fought through some brambles at the end of his run and got back without meeting anyone. He forced himself to be calm as he exited the parking lot. He again pulled off before reaching the entrance ramp, but this time to make the emergency call.

"We've already been notified," Norm was told, "but thank you for your concern. Help is on the way."

⊛⊶❸⊰❉⊱❸⊷⊛

"Hello."

"Norm?"

"Yeah."

"Doreen. You weren't at work today."

"Called in sick."

"Yes. I heard you left a voicemail. You know they don't like that."

81

"Right. My sincerest apologies."

"You sound different, Norm. Are you really sick?"

"Well, it's been a rough couple of days. Day and a half, anyway."

"So you *are* sick."

"Nah, not really. Just a little messed up. Aftermath."

"Aftermath? What do you mean? What happened?"

"Ah, some issues. Coming back from the demo. Just some issues. Then a rough night, drank too much, still sorting things out. Hard to get into just now."

"I see. Well, listen. Maybe I could stop by later. Hear your story in person, share your pain. Maybe I can even help."

Norm hesitated, then: "Nah, it's a guy thing."

"A guy thing?" She laughed.

"No offense. It's just hard to explain right now."

"To me, you mean. Well, let's see. How about McCarten? He's a guy, and he's been a good listening post for you. Patient, discreet and all."

"McCarten. Yeah, that might work. That could help."

"I'll call him for you."

"Okay. And thanks, Doreen."

⊕⊹⊱⊰⊹⊱⊰⊹⊹

I arrived at Norm's apartment building feeling uncomfortable. Doreen's request had seemed strange, the reasons for it vague, but I respected her concern. She'd known us both since we'd started with the company a few years before. I considered her a sincere person, serious, though with Norm my relations usually ranged between bantering and conviviality. It was hard to envision some unusual and grave situation on which he'd want to consult me.

I found him in bathrobe and slippers, smoking and drinking

coffee, the television tuned to a news station with the sound muted. The archetypal worrier.

"Looks like you're up against it," I ventured.

"Yeah, well, it's bad as it looks, or worse."

"So, do we waltz around or do the heart of the matter?"

"Do the heart. But it takes a while to get at."

"Journey of a thousand miles, etc."

"Want some coffee?"

"Guess I'd better."

After I'd gotten a cup and settled in, Norm launched into his tale. It wasn't a smooth telling, however, as he often looped back to cover details he'd missed, altered or repeated things, tried to fill in gaps, was unsure, then emotional and broken. I'd never seen him this vulnerable. I did not interrupt and was impressed.

"I couldn't save her," he said.

"No, you couldn't."

"Flicked on the news soon as I got in. Been watching ever since. Nothing. I can't understand it."

"Tried all the stations? Nothing even similar?"

"Uh-huh."

"What about on the Internet?"

"Not last I looked. But the news stations would have it first, anyway."

I didn't know what to tell him. It was strange to me, too. And coming on top of his catastrophic experience. My eyes drifted to the television until he called me back.

"McCarten."

"Yeah?"

"You up to a favor?"

"Sure, Norm. What can I do?"

It was then that he laid it out for me. He had to know where he stood, what was going on, but there was no way he could go back there or contact the authorities. He might well be recognized or questioned, say something he wasn't supposed to know. So he wanted *me* to go instead, act like I'd just stopped for lunch, ask why the police tape and such, look around. Later I'd report to him at his apartment.

"No phone calls," he specified.

I was inwardly hesitant, of course, but seeing the state Norm was in I couldn't turn him down. I believed his account of what had happened, saw him as blameless in it. And no viable alternative was apparent to me.

"Okay," I agreed. "I'll do it."

⊕⋈३⋈⊱⋉⋅⋸⋈⊷

I left the following morning, taking Route 78 to the state road where Norm had exited. Approaching the area, I paid attention to advertisement signs, thinking I might see a mention of Chun Ling's. A mini-billboard announcing amenities came into view. There were five businesses listed, though Norm had said he'd seen three, and Chun Ling's was not among the five. But Norm had approached from the opposite direction, I realized. He'd seen a different sign. There could be a separate fee for each direction. Yes, I thought, that must be it.

At the base of my exit ramp, I turned left and drove under the highway to where the gravel road branched to my left. I turned onto it, not surprised that the advance sign for Chun Ling's had been removed. I slowed, however, while passing the mini-mall to my right. I stopped. I saw the antiques store on the near end of the strip, as Norm had indicated, but there was a real estate office occupying the unit next to it. Only the furthest two were vacant. This was a clear anomaly. However, I reasoned, Norm was still in a muddled state when he gave his account. While it was replete with details, some might be incorrectly recalled.

I continued down the gravel road.

84

There were more trees and bushes crowding the road than I'd imagined from Norm's account, so the building seemed especially isolated when it suddenly appeared on my right. What distracted me more, though, was a large but flimsy-looking wooden sign that was held on the roof by supports on either side. The supports were higher than necessary so that the word on the sign, *FIREWORKS* in thick red letters, could be read from the highway. I myself hadn't noticed it since I'd approached on the opposite side and had been watching for my exit ramp.

I pulled in and parked where the gravel widened in front of the building. Mine was the only vehicle in sight.

As I got out and approached the building, it occurred to me that there was no police tape or other sign that they'd been around. I also hadn't seen the name "Chun Ling" displayed, or even the fact that this was a restaurant. I tried the door but found it locked. I noticed that the door was rather beat-up, in need of paint, as was the surrounding doorway and in fact the whole front of the building. Walking around a front corner, I observed a loose rain gutter and another unsightly wall. I peered in a window. Though it was curtained, the fabric was askew and I could see boxes and debris strewn about, folding chairs and a cheap table. There was no sign at all of this being a dining room. Advancing to a rear window, I viewed what might have been a kitchen, though only a sink remained from the needed fixtures. As in the front, there were boxes and debris scattered, here with beer cans in the mix.

By the time I checked behind the building, I no longer expected to see the mobile home Norm had mentioned, and of course it wasn't there. The back door to the building was locked as in front.

I stood for a while in a quandary, staring into the rough vegetation leading to the far end of the mini-mall. It looked barely penetrable, likely filled with snakes and other pests, yet

Norm had moved through it swiftly, twice he said. I saw I was not going to accomplish much here.

Returning to my car, I drove further down the road seeking evidence of a crash and fire, but there wasn't any. I turned back and drove past the supposed restaurant to the strip mall. Parking squarely in front of the antiques store, I tried to organize my thoughts so I could ask productive questions. It wasn't easy. I was beginning to feel that Norm had handed me a puzzle and, while I didn't believe it intended on his part, the confusion I'd seen in him was being transferred to my own psyche. I got out and approached the store entrance.

An old-fashioned bell over the door signaled my arrival. The store was somewhat larger than I'd expected from Norm's account, with wooden furniture items predominating. No one was about at first so I browsed, trying to look casual, listening to sounds issuing from an apparent workshop at the back. The sounds continued when a woman of fifty or so came out and asked if she could help me.

"I was looking for Chun Ling's," I answered, "a restaurant someone told me about. I checked down the road just now, this gravel road, but it wasn't where I expected. There was just a fireworks place, nobody in it."

The woman had been smiling but now her smile flattened. She hesitated before responding, eyed me closely.

"You're the second one this week," she said.

"The second one?"

"Mm-hm. Asking about Chun Ling's."

"Asking for directions?"

"Asking what happened. At least the other fella was. Got all upset when I told him. Chun Ling's closed almost two years ago."

My face must have shown my confusion. Her own produced another smile.

"You won't get upset with me now, will you?"

"Oh no, ma'am. I'm just looking to have lunch."

"Good."

"But, I wonder, do you know why they closed? Chun Ling's? I heard they were pretty good."

She shrugged.

"I think business was just bad. The recession, you know. He was saying he might go back to Hong Kong."

"Really? Quite a move. Did he have much family?"

"One or two daughters, I think. Another man was around there sometimes. Don't know if he was a relative."

I briefly considered asking about the daughter or daughters, but decided I shouldn't pry. It might arouse suspicion in the woman and it seemed she didn't know much, anyway. And asking if one of the daughters had been beautiful would be ludicrous.

"There's a hamburger place on the state road here," she said, "about a mile east."

"Oh?"

"For your lunch."

"Oh, yes. Thanks, I'll give it a try."

I turned things over in my mind while having a sandwich, trying to make sense of it all, but without much success. All I could see was that Norm's problem wasn't what he'd described to me, what he perhaps believed. And yet there was something critical at the heart of it. He was not given to prevaricating, or to worry over trivial matters, and he respected our friendship too much to send me off for no purpose, perhaps to be embarrassed. All I could do, I decided, was confront him with what I'd found, however difficult the result.

Back in my car, I decided to call Doreen before driving off.

I'd called her the previous night after seeing Norm, relaying his story to her. She should know now what I'd discovered.

"So none of it ever happened?" she asked incredulously. "He just made the whole thing up?"

"I'm just saying what I saw and heard."

"But why? Why would he do that? And his illness, is that all phony too?"

"No. No, I don't think so. There's something going on, I just don't know what."

A hesitation. All quiet on her end.

"Doreen?"

"Still here."

"Thought I'd lost you."

"Actually, I got this email today. From the client Norm was visiting. Seems he had some problems up there. Wasn't functioning, they say, acted like a zombie. Things got ugly. It's basically a complaint, Jake."

"A complaint?"

"Yes."

"But I thought he was good with them. He'd seen them before, hadn't he?"

"Not for two or three years. They were *my* client, actually, before I got promoted. Norm took my place a couple times when we were going together. Nothing to do with now, of course."

"Right, nothing to do."

I took a moment, tried to envision the past.

"Jake?"

"Yeah, I was just thinking. Norm would've gone by this restaurant, Chun Ling's, those times he filled in for you. It was still open then. Did he ever mention stopping there, or some place like it?"

"No, not a word."

Of course he wouldn't, I thought. Not to his then-current

lover. Not with his impression of the hostess, which I hadn't told Doreen about.

"Did he act any different right after those trips?"

"Let's see. No, I can't say he did. Although—"

She hesitated.

"Yes?"

"Well, after the last one, it wasn't very long before—well, things fell apart for us."

"So there *was* some difference in him."

"More like *in*difference, about us I mean. He'd act distracted, be away from me more. You wouldn't have noticed, I guess. He might even have seemed jollier to you."

I felt caution kick in. I didn't want to go down their personal trail.

"Then, of course, you were promoted."

"Yes. I suppose that sort of sealed things."

"Uh-huh. Well, look. I have to go back to him now. I think it'd help if you were with me, Doreen. Together we might give him some perspective, a more rational view. That is, if we want to stick by him on this. So, how about it? Can you come with me?"

"Yes," she replied with only slight hesitation.

"Okay, I'll pick you up."

❦❧

We arrived at Norm's apartment building in the late afternoon. There was no response when we rang his bell, or when Doreen called him on her cell phone. I'd left mine in the car. For a moment I considered going for it, thinking he'd respond only to me, but this was preempted by Doreen.

"I still have a key," she said, and opened the lobby door.

We climbed the carpeted steps to his apartment. Doreen

started to use her key again but noticed the door wasn't locked. She gently pushed it open.

"Norm?" she called.

No response.

"It's Doreen! I'm with McCarten."

Still all quiet.

"Better let me go first," I said.

We went through the living room, where the television was now off, and past the dining room, where Norm's computer was set up. We saw that the bathroom light was on with the door wide open. There was a small bedroom used for storage and the master bedroom familiar to Doreen, who now gaped at the mess we found there.

"My God! What hit this place?"

Clothes and other items littered the room in complete disorder. Drawers hung open, closets looked rifled. There was broken glass and a smell of liquor. Doreen, stunned, began picking things up while I wondered what had been going through Norm's mind, if in fact he was responsible for this. But then, remembering revelations on the country road, I saw no other explanation.

"I'll look around in the other rooms," I said absently.

The bathroom was also cluttered, but within rational norms, while the room used for storage was actually neat. Once-useful items from Norm's past lay piled in boxes and packages, or covered with plastic. I moved out toward the front of the apartment. I noticed that the computer chair was pulled out from the console and facing to one side, exactly as Norm would have left it when arising from his last session. I approached it thinking to push it in. My attention was arrested, however, by a loose batch of printouts to one side. They were tables of data with notations scrawled in Norm's hand. I sat in the computer chair and examined them.

"Found anything?" Doreen called from the bedroom.

"Still looking!"

The tables on the sheets contained travel information: airline flights, hotels, car rentals. Some of Norm's notations were financial calculations, but more were computations of elapsed time for multi-stop airline flights. He'd apparently tried to piece something together that was better than the itineraries offered. The final destination for both those and his own efforts, however, was always the same: Hong Kong.

Then I saw it: a faint and blurred copy of a document he'd no doubt printed again to get a better image, one that would be usable if a need for it arose. The document was a birth certificate. The name of the newborn child was Norman Chun, the date of birth about two years past.

I sat back heavily in the computer chair. I glanced reflexively toward the master bedroom, the sounds of Doreen cleaning up. I wondered how I should approach her with this.

THE OBSTACLE

Though he was a nervous sort who often exaggerated dangers, Walter should have been able simply to navigate a busy street. Granted, he was in a strange city, and in his pocket was something new and exotic to him. But he needn't have become so confused by the striding throng, by the three oncoming police officers–two hefty males and a diminutive female–that he'd suddenly turn into the first entrance available. If he'd just kept on walking he would have been all right.

As it was, he found himself in a fancy women's clothing store. Thinking it was a standard department store, he looked about for a more appropriate haven, but it was all women's things as far as he could see. He was still gawking about when a svelte, fortyish woman with a manager's badge approached him. Walter cringed a bit inwardly.

"May I help you?" came the standard greeting.

Though he was a nervous, apprehensive person, or maybe because of it, Walter always had a story ready.

"Yes. Hello. I'm just here to pick up a dress for my fiancee. I mean, she already bought it. She left it for alterations."

"Oh? What kind of dress is it? Maybe I saw it back there."

"It was–she said it was a cocktail dress. Maroon, I think she said."

The manager looked him over, perhaps involuntarily. Walter

was gangly with floppy hair and moustache. He was wearing a soccer jersey and jeans.

"Let's go have a look for it," she said. "The name on the order was–?"

"Canterbury."

She stepped off briskly down a main aisle. Thank God she hadn't asked for his I.D. or credit card, Walter thought as he followed, but she would. As the manager began humming to the muzak, he turned sharply into a small side aisle and scooted toward the side of the store. Staying hidden, he slipped along the featureless wall until he came to a double doorway. He quickly went through it to clinch his escape.

He found himself in a very large storeroom, racks and piles of clothing in the area where he stood, large boxes farther back. Advancing inward, he found the passages between the boxes and debris to be irregular, almost a maze, with no clear view toward an exit. He warily tried to stay in one direction, seeking another wall. He came to one but it was a dead end. Retreating, he took another passage that branched off into the dim unknown. By this time there were pieces of furniture interspersed with the boxes, old price tags still attached. The items were very dusty and seemed cheaply made. As Walter continued, the furniture briefly predominated before giving way to cartons of paperback books, many piled high on wooden pallets. Upon inspection, Walter found the books to be over two decades old.

He eventually came to another wall, this time with a shipping and receiving door. He tried the release button but got no response. The mechanism was apparently disabled, with no lift truck present and no signs of recent activity. The dress store apparently received goods elsewhere, perhaps through the double doorway Walter had entered. He now explored further and found a standard door leading to the same alley or minor street as the disabled door. Unfortunately, a huge, heavy wooden crate had been shoved against the door as if to discourage its use. The contents of the crate were identified in black stencil as *Used Books*.

Walter considered his situation. It appeared the immense storeroom had no egress, that he would have to escape through the dress store. But if he went back that way, he might be nabbed for trespassing or attempted theft. Police would be involved. The substance he was carrying was legal in this state, which is why he'd come here, but it would still go on the police report. He'd freaked from habit when he'd seen the three officers and now it was costing him. So he couldn't go back just now, he'd have to wait. This area where he stood, with its forgotten junk from past store tenants, should be safe enough until closing time. Then he'd return to the deserted store and exit the way he'd come in.

Since the store would remain open for some time, Walter sought to make himself comfortable. He managed to find a couch with plastic covering amidst the abandoned furniture. He removed the plastic and stretched out, considered using the substance he'd purchased. He decided it would be reckless in this situation. But since he quickly grew restless when idle, needed distraction to placate his nerves, he got up to select a book from the piled-up cartons. He settled for one called *Escaped Priest*. The title character found his superiors unsympathetic to his personal problems, fled the seminary in the middle of the night, and struggled to fulfil himself in a new life. Walter was attracted by the grainy photograph on the cover, showing a youngish man with a woman and two children, a large broken cross inserted behind them. Walter was soon absorbed in melodrama, forgetful of his own crisis, and fell asleep there on the couch.

He awoke to near-darkness and dead quiet. He slowly recalled his situation, many details fuzzy, and sat up in the gloom. Escape through the front doors, that had been the plan. He stood but stayed bent to feel objects in his path. He picked his way past furniture items and cartons of books, tripping on protruding wooden pallets, cursing the disorder. He eventually came to the clothing racks, the double doorway he'd entered. He passed through it into the store.

Walter was actually in his element now, his job back home being security guard in a museum. The subdued but adequate lighting, the well-ordered aisles, the civilized ambience were all pleasantly familiar to him. But he had no illusions. His position here was indefensible and so he mustn't linger. He proceeded stealthily to the front of the store, wary of its own possible security guard. They wouldn't use dogs around women's clothing. He came to the inner doors and breezed through them, anticipating freedom, then pushed on the outer doors and found them securely locked, both ways.

For God's sake, Walter thought, it's just women's clothes! Before that tacky furniture, before that books of all things! Who wants to steal crap like that? But that was his museum self thinking, he realized. He also knew that he couldn't keep standing there, staring out at the street disconsolately. There weren't many people there now, but patrol cars would be making the rounds. He had to retreat into the building.

He checked an entrance on the far side of the store but found it also well locked, with chain and padlock added. Beyond was a small side street to which the shipping door would have opened. And then, Walter reflected, there was that plain single door with the big crate against it. If he could somehow move that thing, the small door would probably open out. But there was no lift truck or other such assistance. And the weight was just too much for him. But wait a minute. "Used Books." If he could get some of them out–if he were willing to break into the crate–then his problem would likely be solved. He could be extra careful, repack the crate after he moved it. It would be as if he'd never touched it. It'd be in a slightly different position, but that would probably not be noticed.

There were some tools lying about just inside the storeroom, near some mannequins and other display materials. Walter had noticed other tools next to the shipping and receiving door. He couldn't find a crowbar, but he found a heavy duty hammer and large screwdriver that he could use to pry the crate's nails. He was tempted by a short-handled axe on the wall by the shipping door, but stuck to his commitment to inflict no damage, to remain blameless.

The nails, it turned out, were easier to remove than Walter had expected, as if the crate was very old or had been reused, nails previously removed and replaced. A sizable opening was quickly achieved. There was some sort of packing material, something like scrap cork, cushioning the crate's contents. Walter wondered why such care had been taken with used books. He reached in, burrowing through the cork, taking care to avoid a mess. He did not soon feel the smooth and linear shapes of assorted books, however, and doubted that he would, because he felt something much different. It was hard and irregular, with the shapes of ears on top, something linear imposed on the long face beneath. A horse's head with bridle, probably in bronze judging by the feel. Walter had segued into his museum persona.

Climbing down, he reconsidered his action in light of the new discovery. He could still move the crate if the objects within weren't too heavy to lift out. There was the issue of the cork packing, its potential mess, but he could spread furniture covering and dresses on the floor as tarps. But first he'd remove some more boards from the crate to gain some elbow room. There was plenty of time, at least.

He was soon back on the crate digging into its contents. He tried to free the horse's head from the packing and lift it out, but found it wouldn't budge. It occurred to Walter that it might be part of a larger mass. He dug around some more and found the shape of a human head not far behind the horse's, facing in the same direction. Walter was stunned, realizing that this was the rider of the horse, that they were joined in a single bronze sculpture, massive and impossible for him to move. He couldn't quite accept this, however, desperation taking hold, so he dug away more cork to verify the evidence. He soon saw the surface of the face, covered with rough verdigris, and knew it was very old, ancient. The features were strong yet serene, with full beard and thick curly hair. Walter knew from his museum work that the man would be in military attire, his horse also, and Walter knew which army, because this was Marcus Aurelius, second century emperor of Rome. The statue was missing from the Capitoline Museum there, with a standing reward of 100,000 euros for its return.

Walter again climbed down from the crate, his escape stymied but now of little importance. The gaining of the reward was now paramount. It was instinctive: the vision of a prize and the urge to obtain it. But his thoughts were awhirl and he had to have a plan, he couldn't screw up, his nerves and fears had to be controlled. He stood staring at the floor coverings with their scattering of cork chips, waited for his inner turbulence to settle. The night was dead quiet, the side street beyond the door apparently trafficless.

Gathering the fragments of cork, Walter replaced them in the crate and sealed it, tapping the nails into their original holes. He shook out the dresses and furniture covering and returned them also. He put back the tools. Satisfied that all was as it had been, Walter resumed his position on the clean-enough couch, determined to simply exit the storeroom and the store proper when it opened in the morning. If he were noticed, if there were questions, he'd say whatever came to mind and keep walking—fast. He had a reward to claim.

He awoke to the muted patter of daytime and subtly increased lighting. Sitting up stiffly on the couch, he waited for his present reality to come into focus. He had a plan, he recalled, he'd been confident in it. That's why he'd slept soundly. The simple details now came back to him.

When he felt sure he was ready, Walter got up and picked his way back through the dusty furniture and large storage boxes. He slowed as he came to the piles and racks of clothing near the double doorway leading to the store. There was a man working among the spare racks and display materials. He was softly singing to himself as he twisted tubing, rods, and wires. A cup of coffee steamed among the man's tools on a nearby work bench. The store had probably just opened, Walter thought. The man working, in overalls and middle-aged, looked unthreatening. A quick, confident exit should do the trick.

"Hey, what's happening?" Walter smiled as he passed.

"Made it in, man," the worker shrugged. "Good for now, I guess."

Walter pushed through the double doorway and strode through the now-bright store, eyes front. It was indeed early with hardly anyone about. As he turned sharply into the main aisle, however, he saw the svelte manager from the day before, talking with a sales clerk. The manager was facing in Walter's direction and noticed him immediately. She was between him and the exit doors, his escape and passage to riches. His walk slowed a bit but he forced it to stay steady. This was not a time to relapse into fear.

"You're back," the manager said.

"Yes," Walter replied.

He'd stopped, it seeming risky to just brush by. The sales clerk, a young woman, waited mutely.

"I guess we lost each other yesterday," said the manager.

"I took a wrong turn. Then I noticed—it occurred to me—I was in the wrong store."

"To pick up the dress? For your fiancée, wasn't it?"

"Yes, that's it."

Walter caught himself nodding eagerly, smiling widely. The manager frowned a moment, the sales clerk looking confused. He had to control himself.

"Well, thank you for letting us know. I hope you didn't make a special trip."

"No, I didn't."

"Good." A hesitation. "I guess we're done."

Walter gratefully took the cue and strode faster than ever to the exit doors and through them. Once on the street, he took a moment to acclimate himself, then struck off in the direction he'd been taking the day before. The pedestrian traffic wasn't heavy yet, so he was able to see ahead for some distance. He caught sight of the three police officers he'd avoided the day before. They were standing around a corner mailbox, drinking coffee and kibitzing. Walter again felt reflex panic, but only for a second this time, sensing opportunity now where he'd once seen danger. This trio could be his first responders, create a record of his find and a clear basis for his claiming the reward. Why wait? Some shady middleman might try to grab it away from him.

"Excuse me, officers," he addressed them. "I want to report some stolen property I found."

The two male officers exchanged looks and waited, but the short policewoman showed alertness.

"Where is this stolen property, sir?"

"In a storeroom down the street here. It's a priceless ancient sculpture missing from Rome, Italy. I work in museum security and saw the report from Interpol."

The police looked impressed.

"May I see your I.D., sir?"

He showed her his laminated card from the museum. The others looked in and they exchanged brief comments.

"All right, Walter. Lead us to it."

They proceeded along the street while one of the male officers called their station. The other pedestrians cast curious glances, which normally would have bothered Walter, but he was inured to them now by his vision of success. They came to the clothing store and entered, Walter in front. There was no one in sight but the young sales clerk who'd been talking with the manager. Walter breezed by her and down the main aisle, though behind him a male officer bid the clerk good morning. The group wound through aisles and arrived at the double doorway leading to the storeroom.

"Right through here," Walter said, and turned to enter.

But the female officer caught his arm.

"Hold on a sec," then over her shoulder: "What do you think? No words on the door."

"They're coming now, anyway," a policeman replied.

A portly man in business suit was hastening through the aisles toward them, followed by the svelte manager. A sizeable gathering now assembled at the doors, while a higher volume of singing rose from the working man inside.

"I'm Mr. Philpot, site manager," the portly man intoned. "How can I help you, officers?"

"We have a report of possible stolen property back here," the policewoman said. "We need to check it out."

Mr. Philpot winced at the mention of stolen property, but readily gave his consent, also explaining that much in the storeroom was from previous lessees, so he had no knowledge of their origins.

"We won't be long," the policewoman assured him. "It's just one thing and we know where to look." Then to Walter: "Right?"

"Right."

The svelte floor manager had been eyeing Walter and now began apprising Mr. Philpot *sotto voce*. They trailed the officers and Walter as they burst into the storeroom, surprising the singing workman. He dropped the clothing rack he'd been holding and showed the palms of his hands. The group charged past him, led by Walter.

"It's all right, Joseph," said Mr. Philpot. "Just keep working."

They advanced along the irregular passages between storage boxes and debris. Walter slowed at times, considering his direction, but was reassured as first furniture and then book cartons predominated. As they arrived at the back wall with its huge immoveable crate, he felt a glow of triumph and smiled widely.

"There it is," he proclaimed. "The missing Marcus Aurelius. Right in that crate."

The group peered at it bemusedly.

"'Used Books?'" said the policewoman.

"A clumsy ruse," Walter responded.

She nodded, looking back at the crate.

"Julie," said one of the policemen, and he beckoned to her.

They briefly conferred in low tones, the other policeman standing apart. Policewoman Julie then returned to Walter.

"How do you know the statue is in this crate?" she asked. "Was it pictured or described like this in the report?"

"No," said Walter. "I've seen it in there."

"You mean—have you opened the crate?"

"Yes, then resealed it same as before."

"Resealed it."

"Yes."

She looked away from him, back toward the crate, clearly thinking. Her eyes moved toward her colleagues once, but she didn't turn to them.

"Mr. Philpot!" she called.

The site manager stepped forward.

"We'd like to inspect the contents of this crate. Can you have it opened for us?"

"Of course, officer. I'll call our engineer."

He took a walkie-talkie from his belt and spoke forcefully to the man named Joseph. The workman appeared about a minute later, carrying hammer, screwdriver, and small lever. Walter had positioned the stepladder he recalled using himself.

"Please be careful," he said to the workman. "There's a precious museum piece inside."

"I'm always careful," Joseph responded, and went about his task in businesslike fashion, testing the stepladder for stability and such.

Walter felt perfectly relaxed and couldn't help smiling in this, his moment of triumph. It was rare for him to feel pride, he reflected, pride about himself or things he'd done, but this was a time he definitely felt proud. He basked in it. He absorbed the glory of the moment as he watched the workman clamber up, test connections, discover how the nails could be extracted.

"Whoa! Near fell off."

"Be careful, Joseph!" Mr. Philpot implored.

"Yes, sir. Sure will."

He took his time but made good progress after the first board was loose. The group below waited in near-silence. When Joseph had achieved a sizeable opening, he relaxed a bit and peered into the crate. He reached in, seeming to dig through some contents, and frowned.

"Do you see the museum piece?" asked the policewoman.

Joseph glanced down, his expression vacant.

"Got enough here for a *hundred* museums!"

He then proceeded to flip handfuls of small books down to his onlookers. They picked the books up and examined them, found them to be soiled, well-worn textbooks for the primary grades, not very noteworthy except for the inscription stamped on each of them:

For Minority Use Only

It was on the edge of each book's pages, so it could not be covered or easily removed. To try would simply call attention to what had been there.

Walter stared at the book in his hand, then at the crate,

befuddled. What had happened? What was happening now? The others were recovering from their surprise, starting to stare at him. He looked behind to escape their looks, the encroaching guilt and humiliation, mentally fled through the pallets of book cartons, the jumble of old dusty furniture. And of course he stumbled on the answer.

He'd stretched out on a couch *to await the store's closing*, considered using a substance but decided against it. Then he'd felt restless, needed distraction, so he'd selected a book and fallen asleep in the midst of its melodrama.

And there he'd lain until the sounds and light of morning awakened him.

IN THE MONOLITH

The morning had brought mixed results in Richard's investigation. Eva had been of great assistance in talking with the child, a victim of scalding. But despite her expert use of dolls in re-creating the incident, little Kevin had remained evasive. The trauma and fear had clearly run deep. When they'd finished at the hospital, however, Richard treated his coworker to lunch, and together they'd restored their spirits for the afternoon. He dropped Eva at the office before continuing on, warmed by her presence in his life, grateful for their quiet times together.

Richard had financial and marriage problems, but he was relaxed and confident as he drove to his next stop. Investigation was still an escape for him, especially when he worked with Eva. The feeling continued as he arrived at the Novatron offices, for the building was couched amidst lawns and trees, unintimidating. It was, however, a large building, and once inside he braced himself. He remembered the petition in Probate Court and knew the power of Ian Lewing. The name was absent from the wall index, but there was an entry for *Executive Offices*. Richard took an elevator to the uppermost floor.

He came into a waiting room with a large U-shaped couch. A receptionist sat before it, facing inward. Behind her were doors leading to offices. They were labeled with names, but not titles, with one door each for *I. Lewing* and *R. Lewing*. Richard advised the receptionist of his appointment.

"Yes," she said, "Bob's expecting you. But you're early. Just have a seat and go in at ten o'clock."

He sat on the giant *U*, guarded by the receptionist, until a clock on her desk chimed ten o'clock. He was the only visitor there. He knew that Lewing was free to see him, that he should be irritated by the wait, but he couldn't afford that. He wouldn't be swayed by petty, diversionary tricks. Without speaking to the receptionist, he strode to the door marked *R. Lewing*.

"Rick, baby!" he was greeted. "Right on time! Glad you could make it!"

Richard was silent, wary of Lewing's hypocrisy. He took a seat in front of the desk, leaving his briefcase on the floor. The Lewings had to think this was off the record.

"You know what, though, Rick? You should never opt for an office meeting, not when you can get a free lunch out of it. We just write it off our taxes. No sweat. Maybe we can still do it."

"Thanks, but I had a big breakfast."

"Regular bacon-and-eggs man, eh?"

"No. Yogurt and bran flakes."

Lewing laughed, a sudden trill from his Adam's apple.

"Rick, you're a gas! Yogurt and bran flakes, I'll have to remember that one."

Richard felt comfortable. His chair was of leather, well cushioned. He crossed his legs and the chair moved with him, lifting him as he talked. He decided, though, that he'd better start directing things. He shouldn't let Lewing divert him.

"Bob," he said, "I don't want to be blunt, but we both know why I'm here. I'd like to know what's behind that petition, the one filed by you and your father."

Lewing moved in his chair, assumed an aggressive stance.

"Look, Rick. I could go to that door and have *my father* step in and tell you about the petition."

He pointed to a connecting door between their offices.

"But, I say *but*, are you really sure you want to know about it?"

He continued before Richard could answer.

"I mean you could go along and do your work on this thing, and my father could follow through on his thing, and no one would be the wiser. Whatever wound up happening, you would have done your best and no one would give you any problems. But if you start getting into my father's business—well, you're overcomplicating. You can be making more work for yourself, more problems. It doesn't seem worth it, Rick."

Richard frowned, feeling irritated. He knew, though, that Lewing could not dissuade him. It wasn't possible now.

"What do you say?" Lewing asked. "Shall we just forget about it? Go our separate ways?"

"You'd better call your father," Richard replied.

The other man sighed, but quickly got up from his desk.

"Okay, if that's what you want. I always cooperate with authorities."

He left the door open when he went to the other room. There was a murmur of conversation and Richard sat up in his chair. He was beginning to feel tense. When Robert Lewing returned, he was followed by a very tall and broad man with a thick mane of white hair. He moved with grace despite his size, while his bright blue eyes, though penetrating, were warm and sympathetic. His smile was unwavering.

"Rick, this is my father, Ian Lewing. Dad, Mr. Kelsey."

When they shook hands, Richard found that Ian had a loose grasp, despite his obvious strength. He seemed at first a gentle giant, but his eyes suggested a special kind of power. When they were all sitting, Ian ignored his son and concentrated on Richard.

"Well, Mr. Kelsey—Rick, if I may—Bob was telling me you're interested in our Probate action."

"Yes, sir. I am."

"You work for the state?"

"Yes, the Division of Child Protective Services."

He showed his identification plate.

"I'm an investigator, specializing in child welfare."

"Ah, yes. A very worthwhile, very important field. I always wanted to get into it myself. I've done a little volunteer work—playing Santa Claus, coaching a team or two, but I've always wanted to do more. Of course, I've given financially and chaired some drives, but it's the personal involvement that counts the most. I admire you people. I really do."

His voice was strong and resonant, the voice of a senator or evangelist. He was sincere, and Richard had trouble with this. Since he didn't see any falseness, he felt pressured to drop his guard, to trust the man. The beaming blue eyes demanded it. Yet this was his adversary and a man whose past disqualified him. Richard braced himself. He had to be hard, direct, prevent any diversion.

"Mr. Lewing, I've come about the petition you filed in Probate Court, your attempt to get custody of Kevin Castleton."

He looked startled, but in a measured way, as if he knew there was business but preferred small talk. Then he smiled apologetically.

"Yes, of course. You're concerned for Kevin. And well you might be. That's a terrible situation he's in there. Wretched. Abusive boyfriend, mother too weak to throw him out. A boy deserves better than that. He *needs* better."

Richard couldn't disagree, yet he didn't want to encourage the man. Their goals were not the same, after all.

"You must understand, Mr. Lewing, that the division I work for has as its purpose the protection of children like Kevin. We have full authority, under the law, to remove a child or make other plans for him."

The older man just smiled.

"I'm glad you have that authority, Rick. Our abused children need all the protection they can get."

"What I'm saying is that our petition in Juvenile Court takes precedence over the one you filed. It's something they recognize in the court system."

Ian Lewing nodded, looking down. The compassionate eyes were hurt, but not surprised.

"I'm sure," he said, "we all want what's best for Kevin. Surely we agree on that, do we not?"

Richard assented, just to hear what would follow.

"If the boy could be raised in a healthy family setting, where all his needs were met and he could develop to his full potential, that's what we'd want for him. Right?"

Richard had to agree.

"Well, I'm a man of some means, as you may know. Now, when I see Kevin in his current situation—abused, his future up in the air—I naturally look to see what can be done. I was aware, before we filed the petition, of your department's involvement. But I'm also aware of the specific actions your department can take: putting the boy in a foster home, leaving him with grandma Maguire, or—God forbid—returning him to those loonies."

He paused briefly for emphasis. Richard tried to show no reaction, though he was surprised by the man's knowledge.

"As I said, I'm a man of means. So when I look at these alternatives, what the state can offer Kevin, it naturally occurs to me that I can do better. The best education, a fine home, travel—everything he needs to be happy and develop in every way. He'd be secure, a refined young gentleman. Without me, he's left to the winds of fate. And Rick, we both know how many tragic stories there are of children who were wards of the state."

Richard sensed he was being put on the defensive. But the candid, confidential tone of Ian Lewing showed he was speaking to Richard the individual, not Richard the state agent.

"All right," he replied. "I can see you're concerned. But where Kevin goes is still a decision to be made by my agency. If you want to have input in the matter, you should go through us. Or you can file a statement for our hearing."

"Understood. But don't you see, Rick? That's precisely what I'm doing."

"What do you mean?"

"I'm sitting here, talking with you, trying to sell you on what I know is best for Kevin."

Richard was bothered. He'd come for information but was now being worked on.

"Yes," he responded, "but at the same time you have that petition filed in Probate!"

"Don't worry about that. You said yourself that Juvenile Court takes precedence. I'm interested in *you*, Rick. I want to come to a meeting of minds."

Richard tried to meet the beaming blue eyes, the deep wells of confidence, but he found it hard. Many years of success were confronting him.

"What do you think we can agree on?" he asked. "Besides wanting what's best for Kevin?"

The older man smiled with disturbing satisfaction.

"Well, if we agree on what's best for Kevin, then we simply have to decide on how to achieve it."

Richard saw he was rushing ahead, but there was no point in stopping him. He'd hear Ian out for his own information.

"What were you thinking of?"

"It doesn't call for much on your part, actually. You simply report your findings, such as they are, but refrain from making a definite recommendation. You might point out some reasons why Kevin shouldn't stay with the Maguires—their lack of education, accessibility to the abuser, whatever. But also kill the idea of a foster home. Point out that the right relative would take greater interest and provide better for Kevin. That's as far as you need to go. Our lawyers will do the rest."

So that was it, Richard thought. The Lewings wanted Kevin so he, Richard, was a tool to use in getting the boy. But aside from the arrogance of this, there was the question of motive. True to his role as investigator, Richard put his anger aside in favor of inquiry.

"Just why do you want Kevin?" he asked. "I know you said you're concerned about him. But, to take him into your home and be legally responsible, to go after custody—it seems there must be more involved."

To Richard's surprise, the older man seemed moved. He wrung his hands for a moment and glanced over at his son, who had been listening in silence.

"Bob," Ian said, "maybe you should check those materials we were putting together."

Without comment, Robert Lewing rose and went to his father's office, shutting the connecting door. Cooperating with authority, Richard mused.

"He would have stayed," said Ian Lewing, "but it really wouldn't be fair to him. You have to understand, Rick, whatever you think of Bob, that his shortcomings are not a matter of choice. His mother and I gave him everything it was within our ability to give. He was an only child, something beyond our control. And he was a model boy—handsome, athletic, popular. He was good in school, played the saxophone, even read a lot for a while. But there came a time, during college or thereabouts, when we knew something was wrong. It seemed that, somewhere along the line, he couldn't relate any more.

His popularity fell off. Then, after a while, he stopped taking out girls."

He stopped, waiting for Richard's response. But the younger man was committed to listening.

"The last girl he showed any interest in was Kevin's mother, Brianne. Even then he seemed closer to his buddies than to her. When we got the news she was pregnant, it was quite a blow for us. For the wife it was catastrophic. She thought she'd raised the perfect son. Even after things were settled, the heartache stayed with us. After a while, we started thinking in terms of having *another* grandchild, a legitimate one. Maybe it was to ease the memory of what had happened, or maybe we wanted a second chance of some sort. Either way, when it became apparent that Bob, well—"

He broke off, apparently from emotion.

"When we knew we wouldn't be grandparents again, a sort of pall set over the house. Everything we did was tinged with regret, with sorrow for things past. We did the best we could, but the happiness—the hope—was gone. We were well off, of course, but that just made it more ironic, more painful. Then we started to think about Kevin."

Within himself, Richard was fighting against sympathy for the man. It was hard because this was the opposite of his usual approach. And Ian Lewing seemed to know this. He refused to play the role of adversary, which Richard knew he was. Richard felt obliged to remind him where he stood.

"Maybe you should have thought of Kevin before," he said.

"You mean when he was born?"

"Yes."

"Maybe. Of course, we didn't know about Bob then, not entirely. But don't think we only want Kevin because we can't have someone else. Whatever took place in the past, our concern for the boy is genuine. We feel obligated as grandparents to help our own flesh and blood. I honestly believe the boy belongs with us."

He expressed this belief with the gravity of a judge. There was simply no doubting his sincerity. But Richard had to believe Ian was wrong. He had his own convictions.

"What about four years ago?" he asked. "If you're concerned about his being your flesh and blood, why did you go to such lengths to disclaim that relationship before?"

"What lengths do you mean?"

"The arrangement for Gary Castleton to marry Brianne, making your son's friend the legal father. Then you bought them the trailer and paid other people to keep quiet."

The other man frowned, his eyes taking on great intensity.

"Whatever the merits of those charges, Rick, you have to remember I was operating under pressure. Our family life was in turmoil."

"Nonetheless, it would look pretty bad for you in court."

He hadn't planned it this way, but he suddenly realized he had played his ace. His adversary didn't respond but rose from his chair and walked to the window behind his son's desk. He stood looking out, still dignified but not victorious. Richard felt good. He had met the challenge of the powerful man.

"You're right," Lewing acknowledged. "But just *how* bad depends on who brings it up. If anyone. You see, a person isn't likely to make such charges if it reflects on himself."

"You mean Brianne and her parents, the Maguires?"

"Perhaps. But I was mostly thinking of you, Rick."

"Me? What do you mean?"

Lewing came away from the window and stared at Richard from the far end of the desk. He was totally composed.

"I'm well aware of the facts in this case, Rick. I make it my business to know them in anything that concerns me. I know what's going on, and I know about you."

Richard was puzzled but assumed Lewing was bluffing.

"Are you trying to intimidate me?"

"Intimidate a state investigator? Do I seem so foolish? No, Rick. I'm simply stating some facts, which is what you wanted. Isn't that true?"

"Yes."

"All right. You came to hear facts. And I'll give you one now that you already have. It's important that you realize, though, that I have it too. Then we'll understand each other. It involves a young lady, one I met around the time of Kevin's birth. A friend of Gary Castleton. She has a hobby shop now. Do you know who I mean?"

Richard felt his soul cave in. Candace, his wife. He'd kept the case at her urging rather than return it to his supervisor. It was to save his marriage at a slight expense of ethics.

"No," he lied.

"Come on, Rick. I thought you had some class."

Richard met the stare with hollow courage. It seemed to invade his brain, reading every secret under soft blue light.

"No," he repeated.

"She lives at your address."

Richard was silent. The game was up, he thought. He'd lost his big victory, and then some.

"Don't get me wrong, Rick. I'm not going to turn you in. As I told you before, I care about my fellow man. I only wanted you to see that, if we're talking about skeletons in closets, we each have one that the other guy can pull out."

He moved over to his son's chair and sat behind the desk. He picked up an object on the desk and examined it as he waited for Richard to speak. Richard recognized the object as a can of erection prolonger. Ian Lewing threw it in the wastebasket. It occurred to Richard that that he hadn't been defeated by this man. They were only stalemated. And maybe he could break the stalemate, if he were reckless enough.

"Mr. Lewing," he said, "whatever you know about me, I

don't have to do what you want. I can complete my investigation and testify in court the same as I planned to do. What's more, if you try to interfere, I might just bring your skeleton out of the closet and not worry about what you yourself do."

Lewing gazed over the desk at him.

"You wouldn't worry about it?"

"No."

"You'd disregard your future? Your financial security? Your wife?"

Richard felt angry with him, but he had to stay in control.

"I'm committed to the proper handling of this case."

"Oh? Well, don't look now, Rick, but you're into conflict of interest."

Richard recalled warning Candace about it. She'd scoffed, but he couldn't do that. He was the one they'd hold accountable. And, just as Ian Lewing implied, he couldn't ignore the consequences. Lewing had his number and Richard was frustrated.

"Look," said the older man, "whether we like it or not, the best thing for both of us is to work together on this. We both have personal interests that can't be separated from our interest in Kevin. And we're both vulnerable. If we fight each other, both of us will lose and Kevin will lose, too. So the logical thing is to work something out."

Richard was out of arguments. He looked down at his briefcase on the floor, feeling the need to shuffle papers on it.

"I see your point," he said, "but I'm still a professional. I have to do what I think is best. And I truly believe that my plan for Kevin is the correct solution."

"But I feel the same way myself. If I hadn't thought it was best for the boy, I wouldn't have filed in Probate. In spite of my own needs."

"Then maybe we should leave each other alone, keep each other's secrets and let the courts decide."

Lewing smiled grimly.

"Do you have that much confidence in your findings so far? Will they really support your recommendation, stand up to legal challenges? Do you even know for sure what happened when Kevin was hurt?"

Richard answered no, but only to himself.

"The alternative I'm offering, Rick, is something you could easily sell people on, your wife included. We could work out visits with the mother, maybe even the Maguires, so Kevin would still have his social contacts. And you'd be off the hook. You'd have this behind you and could get on with your life. It would be to your credit—a great solution. It would settle the matter with your wife and associates, and it would get you a friend. I can do a lot for you, Rick."

Richard looked up, the gloom in his mind lifting before the beaming blue eyes. Ian Lewing was compassionate, almost fatherly, as he steered Richard's thoughts.

"As I mentioned, I'm a man of means."

Richard wanted to say something about the case, about professional obligations. But the picture in his mind was of his own apartment, the writing table in the corner of the living room, the checkbook with the unpaid bills. He was drained. Ian Lewing had him where he wanted him. Even worse, or maybe better, Richard wanted to hear him out. It was possible he'd misjudged the man, and maybe the whole situation.

"I hear what you're saying," he said. "I guess I could maybe think about your ideas. I don't want to be rigid."

He felt a twinge of guilt as soon as he'd spoken. As he reflected on it, however, the other man made his move. Pressing a button on the intercom, Lewing talked to his son in the next room.

"Bob, did you check those materials?"

"Everything's okay."

"Good. We're coming in now, Bob."

He turned to Richard seeming more at ease, as if matters were settled.

"Shall we move to my office? There's something I want to show you there."

Richard rose stiffly. The chair had been fine but tension had taken its toll. It felt good to stretch his legs, enter a fresh room through the connecting door. He was feeling more relaxed but it wasn't with the confidence, the sense of purpose, that he'd had earlier. Rather, it was a feeling that something good was going to happen, that he was with power here and it was going to help him. Robert Lewing was standing by a conference table, a closed attaché case lying on the polished surface. Richard was lifted by a sense of opulence, the thrill of opportunity, but within him something held back, kept him from committing himself. It wasn't his professionalism; that had been defeated. It was something more deeply rooted on which professionalism was built.

"Congratulations," said Robert Lewing. "You're choosing the right option."

Richard showed a complicit smile. He knew he hadn't chosen anything, but he was curious about the contents of the case. He couldn't help looking at it. Ian Lewing came between him and Robert, laying his hand atop the case.

"Rick," he said, "we have something here to further your career. Not to criticize your briefcase there, but this is handsewn leather, finest quality. It's yours, along with anything you find inside. I think this will make your work easier, and more pleasant."

"Just one big vacation," Robert added.

His father glanced at him sidelong, mildly irritated.

"Bob," he said, "I think we should leave Mr. Kelsey now, let him examine the materials in peace. When you finish, Rick, you can leave by the private exit through that door. It'll take you down to the parking lot."

"Do you have some sunglasses?" Robert asked.

"No," Richard answered, "not with me."

"You can wear these. My compliments."

He laid the glasses next to the case on the table. The green lenses stared up at Richard as the two Lewings turned to leave. When the connecting door had been shut, Richard was left in silence with the case and the glasses, a special door awaiting his passage. Everything was laid out for him.

He sat down.

Springing the latches and hearing a creak as he raised the top of the case, Richard experienced a thrill from childhood. It was like opening presents on Christmas morning. But this was no simple gift, he quickly saw. It was a new and amazing reality. There were bundles of hundred-dollar bills packed tightly, fresh and faded shades of green, degrees of crispness. Old and new and in-between, but all would spend. Richard knew at once there was over a hundred thousand dollars. But as he counted the bundles and calculated mentally, he realized there was well over two hundred thousand. Then he figured more carefully and completely and saw that there was half a million dollars in the case.

He closed it, his heart pounding.

Visions of the effects of fortune flashed in his mind. He saw himself writing out checks, eliminating all debts. He bought expensive items as he would cups of coffee. Rather than have his car heater fixed, he bought a new car—paying cash. He and Candace went out and bought a house. They could afford to have children whenever they wished. He quit his job, working only on his investments. He and Candace ate in fancy restaurants, reveled in entertainment, traveled around the world. Money was like water to them.

Then he thought of the Lewings, his benefactors. Why were they giving him this much? It didn't surprise him that they wanted to buy him, but why had they decided on such a large amount? Perhaps it was a trap of some kind. But if that were the case, what did they have on him? He hadn't signed anything, or even consented verbally. And the payment was in cash. He could pick it up and walk out and no one would know where he got it. No, the Lewings wanted him to have it. The custody of Kevin meant a lot to them and they wanted to ensure they got it. They'd given this much to remove any doubt about his cooperation.

But should he cooperate? He'd come here with a plan and the Lewings were an obstacle. Could he abandon the plan without doing wrong to Kevin? He'd stated his case before Ian Lewing, but the other man had made a strong case of his own. It didn't mean that Richard was wrong. But perhaps Ian was just right enough for Richard to go along. To take the money was self-interest, of course, but there was already conflict of interest, anyway.

He looked toward the exit door, the private exit for escape— escape from the Castleton case, his job as a whole, the pressures of life. Could there possibly be some trick here, a camera or security person? He decided to check it out. He left the money on the table, not wanting to commit himself until he was sure. Trying the door, he found nothing unusual. There was only a stairway leading down, presumably to the parking lot. He could take the money and leave.

Back at the conference table, Richard put on the sunglasses. He started to pick up the attaché case, then hesitated, recalling some people involved in this. He'd already considered Kevin, but he thought now of Brianne, Mrs. Maguire, Candace, and his supervisor. He felt satisfied he wasn't doing them wrong. He picked up the case. He was almost to the door when he stopped.

He thought of Eva, his special coworker.

She, too, would not be harmed by this. She wouldn't be hurt no matter what he did. But the thought of her made the case in his grip feel heavy, the handle slippery. He remembered her help at the hospital, her selflessness. He remembered their lunch that day, their meetings before that, her explanation of her chastity. And he remembered the reason she'd given why she cared for him.

"I respect you for your principles," she'd said.

He felt she was there, looking on calmly as he took the bribe. He could see her dark eyes beneath the dark, wavy hair, and a warm response bloomed within him. He turned back and replaced the case on the table. He took off the sunglasses and put them where Robert Lewing had left them. He wasn't ashamed and somewhat regretted leaving the money, but knew he had to do it. He'd almost made a fortune here, but it wasn't worth the price.

When he was out in the stairwell and the door clicked behind him, he didn't feel so sure of himself. The amount he was leaving and its potential power had a special attraction for him. He decided to have a last look and tried the door. It was locked. He thought of Ian Lewing and knew why the door had locked. Ian had bribed people before; he knew their thinking. He knew Richard would have second thoughts when he was out the door, so the door was fixed to prevent any return. But Ian had thought Richard would have the money and be unable to return it. Instead, he was without the money and now couldn't get it.

Chagrined, Richard turned and descended the stairs. He'd done the right thing, perhaps, and thought he should feel good about it. But it hadn't been his clearly final decision. That remained unmade at the top of the stairway. It would recede in Richard's memory as he returned to his life below, but it would never entirely fade. It would be his sequestered dilemma.

THE SUBCULTURE

In working on his foreign assignment, meeting with contacts of contacts, Peter had strayed or been diverted from his intended course. Official business had segued into existential quest. He now found himself trekking upland with the PLF, passing little skulls set on sticks along the trail. The ground became more level, dipped a bit, and vegetation increased. Below them ran a narrow stream and up the stream were a few huts, the outskirts of a village. They walked toward it through stiff, dry grass.

"You will see some strange things here," said Damian, "but it is best to show no surprise, remain passive."

"For the sake of the alliance?"

"Yes. It can be difficult, but we sometimes must tolerate those less rational. They are a resource. We need to have them fight with us for our goals."

As they crossed the edge of the village, they encountered a group of people standing by the stream. Two painted warriors with long spears stood on the bank, while several women stood in the water. One of the women, a beauty about twenty, was naked and being washed by the others. As the PLF watched, an old man approached Damian and began speaking in the national language. His tone was one of pleasure and excitement.

"He is happy that we are attending their festival," Damian

translated, "but he says we must hurry to greet the elders and have food. The ceremony begins at sunset."

"Why not tell him we were delayed by a panther?"

Damian spoke to the old man, using gestures to describe the incident. The villager looked with astonishment at Peter, then took him by an arm and pulled toward the village. He babbled excitedly, lapsing into the local dialect.

"Here too you will be a hero," said Damian.

They walked in among the huts, which were widely spaced. Against the huts, or in yards between them, were many small idols. Most were erotic in nature. But there were also figures with spears in their backs or knives in their necks, faces contorted with agony.

"What's that noise?" asked Peter.

Sharp, horn-like tones, disconnected and in no apparent order, were issuing on all sides of them.

"They are preparing for the celebration, purifying their huts for the coming of divinity."

"How long does it go on?"

"Until sunset, I think."

They came upon a sizable thatched house with shaded porch. Large pots of flowers lined the porch and next to each pillar perched a bird of paradise. Tall muscular men with golden bolos guarded the entrance.

"This is the residence of the Bok."

"The leader of the village?"

"Yes. Also the supreme living god and center of the universe."

"Are we going to meet him?"

"He never meets with outsiders. He never speaks except to his eunuch, who is also his spokesman, and to one or two servants."

The old man spoke to Damian.

"He says the Bok is meditating to prepare for the ceremony. Otherwise, he would show us his face at a window."

They walked on and passed a group of posts with many small monkeys tied to them. The old man commented on them to Damian.

"These are to be eaten during an interlude in the ceremony."

They came to a large tent with yellow and black stripes. Two middle-aged men were standing under a canopy in front. The guide addressed them and the men greeted Peter and Damian in the local dialect. One of the elders took a large gourd from where it hung by the entrance and handed it to Peter.

"Go ahead. It is a welcoming drink."

He drank and handed the gourd to Damian. It then went back to the elder, who took several gulps and held some of the liquid in his mouth. He seemed to snort a couple of times, then slowly tilted back his head. Coming suddenly forward, he sneezed hard and the liquid exited his nose. Straightening up, he smiled widely and handed the gourd to his companion, who repeated the performance.

"We will go in now and meet the others."

Inside the tent there were more older men and some younger ones painted as warriors. One was especially ornate, with red and blue spikes in his hair and a headband of golden shells. His face was painted white and his body in an arabesque pattern of white, green, and yellow. He stood as he was introduced to Peter, but was silent and showed no expression.

"This is Keelimmin, the general."

"How do you do," said Peter.

The warrior took his hand and raised it in the air. He turned it so that Peter stared into his own palm. The warrior then licked the back of Peter's hand.

"Now you do the same to him," said Damian.

When they left the elders, they were taken to a spot where various foods were displayed under a canopy. Women of the village were shooing away flies. The men of the PLF were invited to fill their bowls, and quickly did so.

"Be sure to take the pork," said Damian. "It will please them. The pig was sanctified before we came."

"How do they do that?"

They sit in a circle around the pig and beckon to its spirit with palm leaves. They apologize to it, saying they do not wish to kill the pig but they must to gain its life. The spirit understands and leaves the pig so they are free to kill and eat it."

"This is quite a place."

"Yes. By the way, do not eat those yellow cakes. The powder on them is dried manure."

"What about the wine we took?"

"Only wine. No problem there."

At sunset, bonfires were lit on the other side of the stream. At first they were kept small, but as darkness set in they blazed unrestrained. People waded across the shallow stream and gathered in a large clearing on the other side. Peter and the PLF joined the exodus. They found themselves in a milling throng that ignored them in the excitement of the hour. Children rang cowbells, old women chattered, and teenage boys chased teenage girls, not hesitating to grab and grope.

As the largest bonfire reached full intensity, blazing like a young sun, a rapid series of jarring booms drowned the noise of the crowd. People fell back from an area in front of the bonfire and a huge, barrel-shaped drum was seen. The drummer's chest glistened with the flames, as did the medallion in the center of his turban.

"It is time for the arrival of the Bok," said Damian.

Across the stream in the light of the flames came an ornate sedan chair, its sides closed. The carriers proceeded slowly and set their load down where the firelight was strong. A semicircle of spectators formed on either side between the fire and the Bok. One of the warriors patrolling the clearing was approached by a chubby young man, who pointed toward the PLF as he spoke. The warrior came over to them and briefly spoke to Damian in the national language.

"He says the rebel leader and the panther killer are to join the Bok at the head of the circle."

They moved to the place of honor, Peter feeling awkward with his pistol still in his belt.

"Isn't he coming out?"

"No. He watches everything through a slit. If he wants a better view, the top of the booth is open."

"He actually stands up?"

"On rare occasions."

A new booming issued from the giant barrel. People fell silent and sharp, flute-like music could be heard, accompanied by the banging of blocks of wood. Six lithe warriors danced into the arena from the end by the fire. They wore round basket lids over their buttocks. They moved to the center of the space and formed a circle, occasionally doing a quick turn but otherwise dancing with monotonous rhythm.

"To do this dance," Damian explained, "you first must kill a man."

The warriors left the way they'd come and four young women flitted into the ring. The flute music played faster and was joined by the jingling of tambourines. The girls were naked but the hair of each was tinted a different color—white, gray, magenta, or pale green. Circles of matching color were painted on their bodies, highlighting physical details. All wore silver bangles on their wrists and ankles that whirled about as they danced. They kicked and shimmied in the center awhile, then faced the Bok and gyrated in place. They formed a diamond with the magenta girl closest. She undulated and snapped her pelvis to the pounding of the giant drum, smiling insanely at the sedan chair. As the drumming grew rapid and the jingling bells reached crescendo, she raised her palms to the stars. Her body glistened with sweat. She and the others grew still then, the flute music the only remaining sound. Finally, turning toward the fire, they ran softly out of the arena.

The next group consisted of a dozen or so young men who scurried into the arena and ran about in all directions. They were almost naked and their faces were painted red, white, and black. Each had a basket of rotten mangoes which he hurled at his fellow performers. They used the empty baskets to hit each other as they ran out, dripping with the sticky fruit. The onlookers laughed with delight, but were suddenly silenced by the huge drum.

A boy and a girl, each about twelve, entered the arena and stood amidst the litter of fruit. The girl was wearing a white gown, the boy a loincloth and large feathers in a headband. For a moment they were motionless, she about two steps in front of him. He folded his arms and she leaned a bit to one side, then to the other. The flute music, slow and monotonous, accompanied her movements. She leaned back, then forward, then at various angles. She leaned farther and farther over, but her feet didn't move.

"What's going on?"

"It is the invocation to the Blue Star."

The girl seemed to defy gravity, swaying to within inches of the ground. She finally raised a hand to the boy, who came forward and helped her from her lowest dip. They left quietly the way they had come.

A fat man and two warriors then entered the arena. One of the warriors carried a spotted dog which he stood on the ground, holding its hind legs. The other warrior raised his bolo and brought it down swiftly, bisecting the dog. The fat man then stepped forward and, raising his arms over the dead dog, said something to the sky. He then squatted before the carcass and, to Peter's disgust, proceeded to consume the inner organs. There was cheering and ringing of cowbells among the onlookers.

"He is the proxy eater for the god," explained Damian. "As I said before, we must make some allowances here."

"Yeah," Peter nodded.

"There will be more sacrifices now. The carcasses become the property of the Bok."

People began to mill around while goats and fowl were killed a short distance down the stream. Thick-set men appeared with trays of monkey heads, each in a tiny basket. The tops had been sawn off, exposing the brains, and people rushed up eagerly to get them. Some of the adults used spoons, but most used their fingers, as if eating from bowls of cauliflower. The chubby attendant of the Bok brought a serving to the sedan chair, lowering it through the open top.

"Are we expected to partake?"

"No, you're safe. I declined once before, so they no longer offer."

Several men with their hands tied were brought before the Bok by the warriors. The prisoners had chicken wings tied over their eyes. They were forced to sit on the ground, where they were cascaded with angry shouts and blows from the crowd. The warriors pushed the people back and Keelimmin, the general who'd licked Peter's hand, addressed the Bok. When he received no response, he turned to his men and gave an order.

"The Bok has judged them guilty."

"Does he ever respond?"

"Only once in twenty years. The accused was an outsider and his father offered many riches."

Two of the warriors picked up one of the prisoners, a teenage boy, and dragged him back toward the fire. Another warrior was heating an iron at the edge of the blaze. The boy screamed in agony as the tip of the iron was applied to his leg, but it was only for a moment. He was freed and two women came forth to attend to him.

"He is marked for life," said Damian. "He must go to the city and wear pants to hide his shame."

"What about the others?"

"We will see."

The other prisoners, three in number, were forced to stand. There followed a long drumming from the giant barrel. Torches were being lit at a smaller fire upstream and people in costumes were gathering downstream. When the drumming stopped, the prisoners were goaded with spears and made to march upstream. A large group of warriors followed. Coming into the arena and following the warriors was the young woman who'd been washed in the stream earlier. She wore a red sarong and strings of coins, shells, and teeth around her neck. With her were about a dozen girls in white sarongs with necklaces of shells, beads, flowers, stones, bottle caps, and knobby black objects.

"Some are wearing ape testicles," Damian observed.

"Who are they?"

"The sacred virgins of the tribe. They were permitted to lose their virginity to the Bok, so now they are sanctified, better than regular virgins. They are given as rewards to the most valiant warriors."

"And the one in front? The pretty one?"

"She has been granted immortality."

After the sacred virgins came a group of people dressed as animals. There was an ox, a lizard, a jackal, an eagle, and a seahorse. The heads were massive, fashioned from wood, and carefully painted in bright colors. A flock of children trotted along with them, the seahorse being the most popular. Next in the procession were baskets of fruit and vegetables. Each carrier had a pole on his shoulder with a basket suspended from either end. A mouse peeped out from a basket of okra as it passed the Bok. The produce was followed by giant erotic effigies, each supported by several villagers. Behind these the rest of the people fell in, shouting with delight and lighting torches. The carriers of the sedan chair again lifted the Bok. As they moved away, an object came flying out the top of the booth. It was the emptied monkey head.

"What if he has to urinate?"

"He does it through the bottom onto the ground."

"Is the ground then sanctified?"

Peter and the PLF joined the procession. It was pushing upstream by torchlight, startling the frogs and small owls that loitered in the night. They passed the village limits and soon the ground was rocky and uneven beneath their feet. Ahead, the erotic effigies bobbed from side to side but the carriers of the Bok kept their burden steady. The ascent became suddenly steep, the torchlit column a glittering snake as it wound up the mountainside. When they were again on level ground the warriors came to a halt. The crowd surrounded a large, dark pit attended by men with long poles.

"It is filled with cobras," said Damian, "perhaps hundreds."

The three prisoners were brought forth and the chicken wings removed from their faces. One by one they were goaded with spears to the edge of the pit, then pushed in. Their screams filled the night and all assembled listened in awe. When the pit was quiet, several warriors approached it and hurled in their spears. A liquid was then poured in and the pit set ablaze.

The ascent was again steep as the procession continued. The carriers of the Bok climbed very slowly along the curving trail. Soon the column came to a halt. In the torchlight ahead, the procession was passing through a narrow gap in the rocks.

"We are at the hot cleft. We must be silent inside."

Damian repeated the warning to his men. They then followed the Bok through the wall and found themselves in a natural amphitheater. The curving wall was white and smooth, as was the floor, which sloped a bit toward a wide chasm in the center. Irregular bursts of steam rose from the chasm. With the light of the moon and the torches reflecting off the white surfaces, it was as bright as an overcast day.

When everyone was settled, the warriors and sacred virgins formed a ring around the chasm. The immortal maiden and the general stood within the ring while the bearers of fruits and vegetables came forward and flung their baskets into the depths. Flute music rose from somewhere in the amphitheater. Peter looked around, then stared in silence at the top of the sedan chair. A bony head was emerging, its eyes fixed on the scene at the chasm, its brows raised in pleasant anticipation. The general had called one of his warriors out of the ring. Making a chair of their arms, the two men hoisted the immortal maiden. They rocked her gently to the solemn strains of the flute, the torchlight fusing them into one fantastic creature. As the flute emitted a strong, high note, the ring of warriors and sacred virgins exploded into sharp cries that ricocheted off the sides of the amphitheater.

"Heeee! Kahee *kahee*! Kahee kahee kahik!"

With a final strong swing, the two warriors lofted the immortal maiden into the steam above the chasm. She seemed to hover a moment, gazing on the stars, then dropped to her death.

All were silent then.

All but one: the Bok, his snicker clearly audible to those around him.

Peter glared at the bony head, disbelief turning quickly to hatred. He fingered his pistol where it hung at his waist. The impulse was rising. He breathed deeply and might have drawn his weapon except that a hand, Damian's, was discreetly restraining him.

"You must not. If you do, we will all be killed."

The clouds of unreason dispelled, Peter relaxed and assumed an innocuous position.

"Of course. Don't worry, I'm okay."

Damian also assumed a passive mien, eyes front, but Peter could sense the other's continued scrutiny, the keen peripheral vision. And when they'd descended the mountain, making their way from the village as its residents continued in revelry, Damian retained an edge of caution. He had the men camp downstream where the immortal maiden had been washed, ordering that no one should leave the camp. A rotating guard was posted. When they bedded down for the night, Damian lay close to Peter. The leader was a light sleeper.

"We will stop a truck for you tomorrow," Damian said, "on the sugar route. The drivers know us and cooperate for their safety. That will get you to the sugar port."

But he couldn't control Peter's thoughts. In them and in levels of dreaming, a much different course was followed. A point-blank shot was taken at the Bok's ear. The top of the head exploded in mid-snicker, leaving it like the monkey heads that had been offered as snacks. It was too good a fate for him, Peter thought, too quick a death. Quicker, no doubt, than his own would be.

While everyone in the dream scene was stunned, reeling from shock added to shock, Peter made his move. He sprinted from his position and ran past the villagers toward the gaping, vaporous chasm. The surface beneath felt chalky, then spongy. He hurtled past the sacred virgins and some startled warriors, believing himself destined for the immortal maiden. His final stride was a long-jumper's, launching himself into the mists of myth and savagery. He tried to view the stars but somehow saw planets, or maybe ghosts of fruits and vegetables. He was falling now, all else closing over him.

He found himself in a dark, soundless oblivion, where he himself was formless, fluctuating toward unconsciousness.

Was this, he thought in the dream, just a dream?

Yes, the mind decided, it must be. For the sake of Damian and his men. For their safety.

THE WINE CORK COLLECTOR

My favorite match, the blond nurse who walks five miles a day, has not responded to my latest communication. We were done with the question-and-answer exchanges, the lists of likes and dislikes and such, so I typed a message in the open format, sent it off by secure email. I tried to be a little more personal but altogether polite and respectful. I wanted to advance our contacts but say nothing that might scare her off. I did take the initiative to suggest an in-person meeting, pointing out the limits of Internet relating. I wasn't at all pushy, though, and left it to her to choose a time and place. I even said we could wait on it if she wished. But still she hasn't responded, even after a reminder note.

It's possible I've been more persistent this time because my membership is due for renewal. I've been indifferent toward most of my matches, so it wouldn't be worthwhile to continue. I'd like to get more for the last fee paid, though. After all, I'm not a computer hermit, content to just pour my thoughts and emotions into a worldwide trash compactor.

Vapors rise from lagoons in my apartment complex as I walk back from the library. Darkness fell while I was sitting in their computer room. The small, scattered buildings have winding walkways between them, infrequent antique lamps that are dim to save energy. Most of the residents here do not walk at night. I'm an exception. It's a place for higher-aged people, designated a "blue zone" for its number of extremely long-lived. The trees have a hovering, threatening aspect in the weak lighting, especially near the vaporous lagoons. It's late autumn and most of the leaves have fallen. Many of the trees rise above the two-story buildings, each of which has three doors, each door leading to six small apartments. It occurs to me as I walk that the complex could be mistaken for mausoleums.

A final turn brings me into the loop of buildings that includes my own. My residence is on a corner of the development, diagonally opposite that which borders the library grounds. I cross the central court, again diagonally, passing parked cars and more trees in the middle, and come to my own familiar door. I hesitate, nagged by non-accomplishment, and look back through the ill-defined shadows. Life is limited, I realize, not only in time but in potential. A person tends to dissolve near the end, swiftly declining in substance and every energy. The past, both the good and the bad, is dead. The importance of now becomes vital, critical, despite one's limitations, because the point approaches at which one completely falls apart and drains into the sewer of non-existence.

<hr />

Having a drink, then another, I gain perspective on my past, explaining and dismissing the shortfalls. The chaos in society, the world, and the mysteries of the universe are explained. Picking up my glass, I move to the patio door and slide it open, exit to the small fenced yard that goes with my apartment. It would be pitch dark without the glow from inside. I stay within the fence, not seeking any encounters with coyotes, skunks, or their human equivalents. I sip and peer into the night, across the little-used road, the privacy fence that borders the other side. It's hardly needed since the backyards beyond are filled with more trees. Very few lights are visible from the houses. To my left are traffic sounds from a larger street, still not so bright since it isn't commercial.

I decide to delete the five-mile blonde from my active matches. Enough is enough in the waiting game. Waiting too much has often accompanied my failures: letting things slide along, putting up with things I needn't, imagining I'm doing a sort of "end run" on life, that I'll eventually do great at the right time, the right place, with the right people. Of course, even if I'd had more success along the way, I still might have wound up here, at Elm Grove Apartments, alone. But that just makes it more imperative, more vital, to take strong action now. This is the closest I'll ever come to finishing my end run.

❧❀❦❀❧

Evening in the library computer room: two dozen setups along the walls and in short rows, four on a pillar for use while standing, chairs in stages of dysfunction. The walls are glass. Here I'm oblivious to all around me as I focus on my matches, new and old and in-between, at various levels of communication. I don't feel strongly toward any of them now, but I like to keep a certain number around, seven or eight or so, as a reserve of hope, resources in case my tastes or criteria change. In case I want to lower the bar, in case I get desperate.

There's one I'm considering as replacement for the nurse. I hadn't thought seriously about her before, letting her flounder at fourth or fifth on the list, but now she seems somewhat acceptable. She's one of the younger ones, sixteen years my junior, and on the short side, ten inches below me, rather ordinary in appearance but physically sound. Her picture shows her in a lunchroom or cheap restaurant, her arms resting on a table, her head tilted to one side and smiling at the picture-taker. She's wearing a sleeveless top, her arms toned well for one in her early fifties. Her hair is a casual bob of indistinct color, dark blond or light brown, and she's rather pale. Her likes include the usual traveling and popular music, novels by female authors and inspirational books, the company of family and friends, and (hopefully) an honest and committed relationship. Staring at her picture, I try to gauge how dull she would be, then suddenly remember that I've got nothing going and need to make a move. I click the link to send her a message via secure email.

❦❦❦❦

I walk with hands in pockets, cap pulled low, along the non-commercial major street near my apartment. It's about three-quarters of a mile to the temple, the meditation room. A few snowflakes blow in the beams from headlights. People are snug in their homes for the night, their lives mostly ordered, structured, goals set and being accomplished, or else failure and defeat accepted. For me, though, it's a different story, a limbo of non-finality. The causes for it are within me, I believe, a mishmash of non-decisive factors. The struggle between approach and avoidance, taking many forms, has led to an amorphous status—socially, professionally, culturally, you name it. I've been dancing on the fringe of human endeavor, a dance that I've grown tired of but see no end to, if one even exists aside from death. But then there's this meditation room. I've been to it before, enjoyed its ambience, felt it contains answers superior to one's own. It must, or why else would the temple maintain it?

I turn at an intersecting street and walk a couple of blocks east. It's darker now. I enter the driveway and pass mostly empty parking spaces, come to the wooden doors and enter, take a side door off the lobby since the temple proper is locked. A short hallway with magenta carpeting opens on one side to the meditation room. It's candle-lit, a fountain softly trickling on one side, the air scented by flowers. A man in robes squats in front to the right, head bowed low. I squat in the rear and to the left. I do not bow.

My new lead match occupies my thoughts. Not so much she herself, her attributes, but her suggestion, which I invited, that we meet this Saturday at Caribou Coffee. I have not yet responded, my natural inclination being to stall, which usually leads to plans fizzling out and my bittersweet relief. Such willful failures fill my memories of past life: reluctance to engage playmates, putting off sports and music activities, negligence toward youthful friendships, avoidance of dating. The images of several young women come to mind, potential relationships offered through introductions but which I spurned. About to become president of the debate club in my senior year, I instead dropped out. Awarded an ROTC scholarship, I left it unused rather than settle for my second college preference. As a senior in college, I dropped a key course required for graduate school, simply because I didn't like it. I later considered different fields—business, law—and obtained information, could have entered them, but always there was the stalling, leaving the follow-through for later. And of course it carried over to my adult relationships, always provisional, failing to move on to what should naturally follow. Even when I presented my feelings as genuine, they were somehow seen as lacking, hollow. Which they were, I knew at some level. Even the most intimate unions were never completely so. There was my reluctance to yield, to stop stalling and give in, to be absorbed in a fully felt commitment. I've been an enigma to people, an odd thing, a pair of ragged claws scuttling across the ocean floor.

A young woman enters the meditation room. She has longish dark hair and carries a box. She quietly tends the candles, replacing a few and straightening others. As she lights one of the new ones with the flame of another, she glances my way, the light soft on her eyes, momentarily feline. She is gone a moment later. Only I and the man in front remain in the room, he again bowing after briefly straightening. My mind is indeed blank now, the past having been dispelled, letting awareness enter. Questions of waiting and stalling are irrelevant. I will go to Caribou Coffee, no big deal, and what happens, happens. I let this sit in my mind awhile, then get up and leave.

The coffee shop is in a sprawling mall in a suburb adjoining my own. Many of the storefronts are vacant, including the largest one, the "flagship." I'm sitting at a table by the windows at the front of the shop. The place is rather busy, mostly with talkative young people. The man at the table next to mine is absorbed in his electronic device. I pretend to read a newspaper as I wait for Sharon, who is fifteen minutes late. I'm indifferent to her showing, a part of me hoping she won't, but there's a tension about this deep within me. I feel dizziness rising as I scan the newsprint, once almost falling off my chair. I catch myself on the table edge.

I think I see her enter, but I don't get up since I thought I saw her earlier and was mistaken. This time, however, I sense her coming up behind me, having taken a moment to scan the crowd.

"Mark?"

I turn my head, then rise a bit awkwardly.

"Yes. Hello, Sharon. Sit down?"

I gesture toward the other chair at our table. She takes it, draping her coat over the back. She looks a little heavier than her picture, but it might be since she's wearing a sweater, and there's the ubiquitous gold cross pendant. Her hair is mussed though she wasn't wearing a hat. She looks cautiously pleased.

"Well," she says, "here we are."

"Yes." I hesitate, my mind blank, then: "Can I get you a coffee?"

"Oh, well, maybe a hot chocolate."

I go to the counter and order it. I sense her back at the table, appraising me. I try to order my thoughts. I have no plan for our conversation, I will have to draw on banalities, though I was hoping for a positive experience from this, some resolution. The cup of hot chocolate arrives. I pay. I take my time returning to the table.

"Thank you," she says, "and I have something for *you*."

I wait as she digs in her handbag, produces a small object that she places at center table. It's cylindrical, purple in color, and picking it up I see it's a synthetic wine cork, the vintner's name embedded on it. I recall that I listed collecting wine corks as my favorite hobby.

"Yes," I say, "I don't think I have this one."

"That's what I thought," she beams.

"Well, thank you."

I turn away to put it in my jacket, hung like hers on the back of my chair. It's going well, I think, but I have to talk, come up with things to say.

"So," I proffer, "have you been in TruMatch for long?"

"Oh, well, no. Just a few months or so."

Her voice trails off as she swirls her chocolate and looks in it. Did I commit a faux pas?

"I haven't been in much longer," I lie. "I guess it's a good thing. I got this one meeting at least, so I guess I can't complain. Right?"

"Sure," she smiles. "Me, too."

I ask if she's lived in the area for long, a safe enough question, and she mentions another suburb she grew up in, a blue-collar community, and its local high school that I'm familiar with.

"I didn't go to college," she states flatly.

"I only had a little," I respond, dismissing the existence of my two degrees.

"I lived in different places for a long time after that. Virginia, Massachusetts, we moved a lot. Things always happened and we moved. Then it was over and I came back here to my family."

I resolve to not question who "we" included.

"Did you like it in Massachusetts? I'm originally a New Englander myself. New Hampshire."

She smiles at the vague commonality.

"Maybe it's nicer there than we thought. We kept running into—"

She uses an expletive, looking away as she does so.

"Sorry," she mutters with a glance back.

I don't react, long steeled against supposedly strong language. I see it as just the opposite: a symptom of weakness in communication skills, and probably in thinking ability. A meaningless word or expression is used to fill a void in personality, perhaps in character. Shock value is relied on to conceal ignorance, shallowness, inferiority.

"I've lived around here since my teens," I say to change the subject, then give a redacted version of my work history. I tell of being an investigator, but omit my later career in teaching. I mention going to court with my findings, but not my frequent reliance on psychological and psychiatric evaluations. I add my early factory jobs as a finisher. Sharon is duly impressed.

"I'm with my father just now," she volunteers. "He's a

dementia patient. Sometimes my sister comes to help out. Mostly, though, it's just us two and the cat. We do the crosswords every day since they said it'd help. I don't know, maybe it does. Better than most of their—"

Another expletive. I see clearly that this is our last meeting. My task in this place now is to extricate myself. A noisy expresso machine has been invading our conversation, further taxing my patience. But I have my standards. I will stay diplomatic with Sharon, smoothly and respectfully get past her.

"That's certainly good of you to care for your father that way. Doing the puzzles with you must make his day. Will he be waiting to do one when you get home?"

"No, we do them in the morning. I do have to get to church, though, the 5:30 service. And then make a stop at Quick Buy. Cat food and stuff."

"Oh."

I inwardly give her credit for limiting our meeting, though she doesn't know it's the end of our relationship. The expresso machine explodes again, opportunely for me now.

"Maybe we should step outside," I say, "talk a little more without that noise."

"Okay."

We don on our coats and wind through tables to the door. It's grown colder outside, the sun low in the west, the sky a sentimental gold. I look down at her and smile, at a loss for something tender, optimistic, to say, prevented as I am by the irony of the situation. She waits expectantly.

"Well," I manage, "perhaps we can get in touch by email in a few days, share any great thoughts about today." I hesitate, then: "It was pleasant."

"Yes," she answers. "For me, too."

"It was really nice meeting you. I think you're *really* a very good person."

An odd, histrionic fervency is in my voice. Sharon's expression goes blank.

"Thank you. I'm sure you're a good person, too."

I simply look at her, my mouth open but stuck for words.

"Well, take care then, Mark." And she edges away.

"Yes. Good-bye."

She halts briefly in her motion, her features stiffening at the word. She continues to her boxy vehicle, parked where we've been standing, throws open the door without looking back. I turn away before we can face each other through the windshield. I walk down the sidewalk to my car.

❦❧❦❧❦

Driving away from the rendezvous, I'm somewhat dazed by the experience. There's the familiar sense of relief, having dodged further obligations, but also a greater comfort, a confidence that I was right. It's better that I end things now, after all, than after seeing her again and again, when the breakup would be more painful for her. I have only the slightest sense of loss, probably of wasted time, and accept the fiasco as something fated, inevitable. Floating along in this mental current, I notice that I've missed my turn, driven well south into the next county. Also, the season's sudden darkness has fallen. I should stop and consult a road map, but don't wish to interrupt my thoughts, so I simply turn and drive in the general direction of where I'm supposed to be.

I drive through an office park, darkened now after the short work day. I park by a lagoon, get out of the car, approach the water's edge. So peaceful it is here. A woman is walking her dog on the other side. They're moving down a paved path toward an apartment complex amid the office buildings. Housing for people who work here, I suppose. I watch the woman fade into the night, thinking how Sharon is no more meaningful to me now than this stranger. And neither are the others, the many I left so awkwardly, mindful of their discomfort but lacking the skill to assuage it. I see their faces on the surface of the lagoon, their bodies, the places and rooms where I knew them. A new rippling crosses the water, intersecting that of the wind. I don't see the source, or hear it, but there are creatures of the night besides myself, I know.

It occurs to me that I can walk into the lagoon right now and end it all. A skim of ice would form by morning, sealing me in, perhaps thicken since days are growing colder. But then there's the road map in my car, another way out of here, a plan. I should be sure before I act. I will turn now and walk away from the lagoon.

❦❧❦❧❦

I sit again in the library computer room, now in the waning days of my TruMatch membership. I'm checking for contact from a new group of matches, having sent them questions after the Caribou incident, wanting to get my money's worth up to the end. Only one of the new ones has responded. I ignore her multiple-choice answers, being quite tired of the routine. All that matters is her showing interest. I return to her pictures, three in number and on the odd side. Two that are almost identical show her standing before a fake fireplace. She faces sideways and has an arm raised in one of the pictures, as if she's reaching for something. She's slender and has a short mop of brown hair. In the third picture she holds a panda doll amid some cushions. I guess she's supposed to look cuddly but, with her gangly build, she just looks goofy.

I decide to send her a secure email, skipping the intervening questions, likes and dislikes, etc. I'll give the impending end of my membership as the reason. While I'm at it, I might as well mention the desirability of our meeting, stressing the limitations of remote relating. The holidays are almost upon us and I'll be out of town, but we can meet afterwards. Perhaps she'll be receptive to this. In any event, I can feel that I'm making the most of my membership, getting my money's worth in my own way.

***

I slip before dawn from the room I'm using to the one with the old computer. The others in the house are still asleep. They have their laptops and so don't bother with this computer, but I use it here for privacy. I look toward the window, the semi-rural landscape in darkness, town and countryside lost in timeless night. It wasn't much different on yesterday's walk, heavy clouds filling the sky and diminishing all below. But here and now I can approximate my world back home, give reign to the narrative of my own thoughts, accommodate its demands as suits my mood. Indulge in illusion, I suppose, or else mock it.

I see Arlene has sent me a message. It's at the new email address that I got just for her, though she doesn't know that. She hopes I had a nice Christmas and looks forward to our meeting after New Year's. She gushes on for a while about new horizons, fulfillment, the meaning of life. She ends by saying she can't wait to be with me. The message is typed in bright red.

I suppose that I should respond. Looking at the text in red, however, something stirs at the back of my mind. I know the color is holiday inspired, but springing at me in this context—time and place and situation—it weirdly amplifies the words of the message. I don't think I can match the apparent emotion. A reflexive sort of caution, perhaps fear, constrains my response. I must remain noncommittal. I thank her for her greeting, describe the weather where I'm staying, say a coffee shop might be best for our meeting. I save the draft to send in a day or two. I don't want her to think I'm hanging on the keyboard with bated breath, eager to exchange sweet nothings.

⊖⊢╞⊰╟⊱⊢⊖

It seems sudden that this day has arrived. I've been to the library computer room only once since my return, minimizing my contact with Arlene. She was agreeable to the coffee shop meeting, leaving the details to me. I selected a Starbucks location in her suburb and made the time two o'clock, earlier than last time to avoid church and cat food conflicts. I'm driving to the appointment now. It's a cloudy, windy day, cold but not bad for early January. I'm apprehensive, of course, part of me hoping she doesn't show up, but the gentleman side of me requires I follow through. I avoided contact after sending her the place and time, so I suppose things were never really finalized. But this just means I'm giving her options, I think. Show or don't show, it's up to you. Whichever she chooses, I'm fine with it, though there's a little leaning toward *don't show*.

The address for the coffee place is in a tackier sort of mall. Since it's Saturday, there's a goodly number of parked cars, but I easily cruise the perimeter and scan the fronts of the businesses. Snowflakes are blowing around now, so I have to squint a bit. I make a full pass but do not see the Starbucks. I'm about to swing around for another look when I spot their sign out by the road. It's free-standing, distant from the mall complex, but nearby is a small, box-like building with its own driveway on the road side. It appears I gave Arlene the address of a drive-through-only facility.

I park in a space and contemplate the coffee structure. What rotten luck! Unbelievable. Not my fault though, I tell myself. The snowflakes are swirling thicker now, not that I'd see much

143

anyway. Certainly not someone standing about waiting for me. A car, then another, arrive and pass the drive-through window, which is on the side of the building facing away from me. I can't make out the drivers' faces. It occurs to me I should get out of my car for a better view of things. Arlene might pop into view and I can flag her down. I open my door and enter the blast of winter.

The drive-through is on a raised concrete island, not far from where I've parked. I walk to the narrowing end of the island that cars pass when they exit. I cannot be seen by the employees inside. From my vantage point, I can see the exiting drivers and anyone near me in the parking lot. As I wait in the swirling snow, I feel rather foolish, but what else can I do? There's a heavy iron door on my end of the coffee structure, which I try but find locked. Now what? I needn't wait very long, I think, to fulfill my commitment, so I'll give it fifteen minutes minus time spent. As the deadline approaches, a familiar sense of relief begins to rise in me, anticipation of another bittersweet escape. I fiddle with the car keys in my coat pocket.

Suddenly, however, I spot a bundled form moving out of the aisle in which I parked, coming toward me. A crazy fur hat with long earlaps is atop the bundling, but there's no mistaking the doll-like face beneath. She fixes me with eager eyes and smile and I feel impaled. I remain on the concrete island as she approaches through the snow, steps up and stands before me.

"So we meet," she says.

"Yes. Sorry about the place. I was just going by the address."

"I figured. Actually, I got here before you. I was keeping warm in my car, then I wanted to be sure it was you."

"Oh. So how did you decide it was me?"

"Well, who else would be standing around here like this?"

"Ah. Yes. Who else?"

We exchange smiles, our ridiculous situation morphing into something logical.

"There's a place down the road here," she says. "Scipio's. Two stoplights west. How about we go there and get out of the cold?"

"Okay."

We return to our cars and I follow her as she winds out of the mall. As we proceed through slow traffic, I'm conscious of having the choice to suddenly turn off and disappear into the neighborhoods. I could return to the library computer room and delete the special email address, as well as any traces of myself on TruMatch. But the crudeness of the action is outside my standards, my capabilities, and I'm also aware of something holding me here. It's a temptation or opportunity to yield to the inevitable, to end a decades-long struggle. Or at least transform it, change it to something separate from myself that I can analyze at leisure, without intrigues. Something I might eventually understand.

I follow Arlene to Scipio's, which has a sign with cartoon cocktails on it. It's 2:30 p.m., the slow period, so we have no trouble parking next to each other. I find I'm looking forward to this. A really fine day might be taking shape.